A star of shattered glass, cold against my temple.

Blackness.

Sinking in the woolly blackness, choking, drowning, suffocating.

I want to claw my way out but can't move, want to scream but don't know how. The blackness is swallowing me and I know that if I can't fight it the me will be gone and the blackness will go on without end.

Strapped on a bed; hard, jolting; pain jabbing, throbbing, screaming.

A woman looming over me . . . smiling . . . blue uniform—*an ambulance?*

'How's the pain?'

Past pain into a new dimension of horror; neck shredded, strangled; spasms from hell.

Something over my face; I can't talk. Have to tell her, make her understand, make her fix it! Squeeze my fist in the air, tightly and rhythmically; desperately. *I can't take much more,* my fist screams.

The woman smiles. 'Not too bad?'

A nightmare. It has to be a nightmare.

But even in a nightmare I'd never make an ambulance so uncomfortable. *This must be real.*

ALSO AVAILABLE IN LAUREL-LEAF BOOKS:

NUMBER THE STARS, *Lois Lowry*
THE WITCH OF BLACKBIRD POND, *Elizabeth George Speare*
A RING OF ENDLESS LIGHT, *Madeleine L'Engle*
WILL YOU BE MY BRUSSELS SPROUT?, *Lucy Frank*
TENDERNESS, *Robert Cormier*
STONE WATER, *Barbara Snow Gilbert*
THE HOUSE YOU PASS ON THE WAY, *Jacqueline Woodson*
CROSSES, *Shelley Stoehr*
NO EASY ANSWERS: SHORT STORIES ABOUT TEENAGERS MAKING
TOUGH DECISIONS, *edited by Donald R. Gallo*
KINSHIP, *Trudy Krisher*
THE WAR IN GEORGIA, *Jerrie Oughton*

PEELING THE ONION

Wendy Orr

Published by
Bantam Doubleday Dell Books for Young Readers
a division of
Random House, Inc.
1540 Broadway
New York, New York 10036

Visit us on the Web! www.randomhouse.com

Educators and librarians, for a variety of teaching tools, visit us at www.randomhouse.com/teachers

ISBN: 0-440-22773-9

RL: 6.0

Reprinted by arrangement with Holiday House, Inc.

Printed in the United States of America

March 1999

10 9 8 7 6 5 4 3 2 1

OPM

For my family
and all my friends—
the ones who stuck by me,
and the ones I met along the way

PEELING THE ONION

CHAPTER 1

I've won. I'm tingling with energy and excitement; bowing to the judges, accepting—it's the first tournament on the way to the Nationals, and I've just fought last year's champion . . . and the golden figure on its black marble stand is mine.

A two-fingered whistle splits the silence; Hayden is waving his fists in the air and shouting my name. I step back into the crowd and his arms go around me . . . the kiss is long and fantastic and I don't think we can say we're just friends any more.

'Save it for the bedroom, you two!' Sensai growls, but I'm too happy to be embarrassed.

A star of shattered glass, cold against my temple.
    Blackness.
    Sinking in the woolly blackness, choking, drowning, suffo-
cating.
    I want to claw my way out but can't move, want to scream
but don't know how. The blackness is swallowing me and I
know that if I can't fight it the me will be gone and the
blackness will go on without end.

Strapped on a bed; hard, jolting; pain jabbing, throbbing, screaming.

A woman looming over me ... smiling ... blue uniform—*an ambulance?*

'How's the pain?'

Past pain into a new dimension of horror; neck shredded, strangled; spasms from hell.

Something over my face; I can't talk. Have to tell her, make her understand, make her fix it! Squeeze my fist in the air, tightly and rhythmically; desperately. *I can't take much more,* my fist screams.

The woman smiles. 'Not too bad?'

A nightmare. It has to be a nightmare.

But even in a nightmare I'd never make an ambulance so uncomfortable. *This must be real.*

The ambulance stops. A mask is pulled off my face. My bed bumps out into fresh air; rolls through swinging plastic doors and past my parents. They're huddled together, cold and shrunken.

I fade out again; open my eyes to a busy, clattering room with white ceilings; an invisible child crying. Faces hover; white coats and nurses. Deft strokes and sharp knives skin me from T-shirt and jeans—new jeans; I'd have worn old ones if I'd known. My tulip T-shirt, Aunt Lieke sent it from Holland. *Did I say that out loud?*

'We'll save the motif if you want—you could soak out the blood and stitch it onto something else.'

Must have. 'It doesn't matter.'

I remember now—Lieke's dead. Maybe it wasn't a lucky T-shirt.

A sheet draped over me; a doctor dabbing something on my cheek. 'You were lucky—a little higher and you could have lost an eye.'

Three stitches. They'll dissolve in a few days.

'Now—how do you feel about cleft chins?'

????? Don't let him see the panic. 'Just what I always wanted.'

'That's the spirit ... this will taste funny'—bitter liquid straight into my mouth from a hole in my chin. *Hole through my chin! Sounds yuck. Don't care.*

Mum and Dad again. Dad sniffs; blows his nose. *Crying?* A huge terrible knowledge lurks under the pain, under this babble of words flowing through my brain or out of my mouth.

'Is this real?' I ask. Nobody answers. The young doctor wants to know who and where I am, what day it is. The same questions they ask when you're hit in the head at karate—can't trick me, I'll answer their questions, I'll be polite—they won't let you fight if you don't. Now a torch, bright as a laser beam into my eyes. Makes me squeal—*smash it away!* Stop myself just in time.

'X-rays,' he orders.

Wheeled into another room—'Lie still!'

What do they think I'm going to do, jump up and dance? I don't ever want to move again.

Back to the noisy, bright room ... like a casualty ward on a TV soapie—*I'm not supposed to be here!* The child is still crying. So are my parents, with sniffs and angry wipes at their eyes.

Smiling faces: whiplash, not a broken neck. *Doesn't broken neck mean dead?* Pain slivers thought. Broken thumb but ankles only sprained—torn ligaments, chips of bone, not serious; one doesn't even deserve an X-ray.

Now Hayden's here with a nurse behind him and someone who must be his mum. His face is whitish-grey; he has blood in his hair, on his shirt. 'Anna, I'm so sorry,' he says, and starts to cry.

I don't want him to cry. It's all too hard. 'It's not your fault,' I tell him, and close my eyes.

CHAPTER 2

I wake in a bed littered with glass. It's morning . . . a hospital ward . . . I'm wearing a foam rubber collar and I'm surrounded by old ladies.

The one in the bed by the window is so old that she's only semi-conscious. I hope she doesn't die today. The others are old but awake: Mrs Hogan is beside me, and in the bed across is Ruby.

I try to sit up. I can't. I'm anchored to the bed by pain. I try again, and yelp like a trodden-on puppy. *God, this is so humiliating!*

A girl appears. *Fiona*, her name badge says. *Student nurse.* 'I'm supposed to do your neurological obs.' She studies the slip of paper in her palm. 'Are you alert and orientated?'

Alert enough to know I'm desperate for the toilet! 'Yes.'

A torch waves like a question mark. 'I have to look at your eyes.'

You're not flashing that in my face again! 'Shine it on the ceiling and watch me look at it.'

She obeys gratefully. Pushing my luck, I ask if she can help me to the toilet. She says she doesn't know, she'll have to ask someone; disappears and doesn't come back.

Peeing must be next week's lesson.

Next is Sister in Charge of Tablets. She clanks with keys, and I think she'll be high enough to know about bladders.

Too high, she's gone right past. The trolley can't be left alone, she says.

'It's not alive,' Ruby mutters. 'It won't escape.'

Tablet Sister ignores her. Do I want something for pain?

Of course I do: arsenic, heroin, I don't care—I'll swallow a handful.

'Please,' I say. But I still need to use the toilet.

Another nurse comes but this is worse, she's got a bedpan—*she can't be serious, I can't use that, it's disgusting—please let me go to the toilet!* She says I'm not allowed out of bed; it's this or nothing.

She's sliding the pan towards my bottom; my right hand is the only part of me not injured, but somehow I have to lift my hips and hop on top, lying down. My neck shrieks. So do I. The nurse is not amused. 'If you'd just relax,' she snaps, 'it wouldn't hurt so much.' She bustles off to bully some other new inmate.

'Busy Butt,' says Ruby. 'Look at the way she flaps it! Thinks she rules the world.'

That wasn't the way I thought old ladies talked.

Suddenly the curtain between my bed and Mrs Hogan's is whipped shut, and the sheet is whisked off my legs. A short, stout grey man leading a crowd of white coats gives me an 'I'm too busy for you' glance and reaches for the clipboard at the foot of my bed.

I'm wearing a short backless nightgown designed by a pervert. I feel as naked as I am. 'Hello,' I say, but only the young doctor from Casualty gives me a quick smile before launching into a coded speech to his big boss, the small grey man.

'MVA, last night,' I pick out from the medico-babble. 'Seventeen years old. Closed head injury; soft tissue injuries to the neck.'

'X-rayed?' barks the god.

'Yes,' says the young one, as he spouts off another mind-numbing stream of gibberish. It sounds impressive. It doesn't sound like me. *Seventeen years old* is the only thing I understand, and I wish he'd stopped there.

Now it's Tablet Sister's turn; she discusses my pain and how I slept. The pain has nothing to do with *me*, apparently; don't mind me, I'm just the body that owns it.

I lie there, legs pressed tight together and my good hand clutching my nightie, as quiet and still as the dummy they want me to be. Suddenly the sheet is whipped back up to neatness; the group turns to Mrs Hogan, and I'm invisible again.

How could this happen to me? Things like this only happen to other people. That's how I know it's not real.

Mum's here. I'm surprised by how glad I am to see her, clinging to her as fiercely and desperately as a child.

She unpacks a bag, a dressing gown, her new blue nightie, toothbrush and hairbrush, deodorant and talc. No mirror. She flusters, says she's lost her compact.

Delicately, tenderly, she begins to comb my hair. Half a windscreen seems to be tangled through it, embedded in every strand of my falling-out braid. The shards plink into the bag taped to the side of my bed. Mum's fingers probe and soothe.

She's still at it when Dad arrives with Bronny and Matt. They hang back, twisting awkward feet at the end of my bed while Dad tiptoes up and kisses me gingerly. 'Come on,' he says, 'show Anna what you've got for her.'

Drawings. Bronny's is a card, with flowers and a black and white cat I recognise as Sally, *Get Well* printed neatly inside. Matthew's is 'You in the ambulance,' he explains, 'and that's the car, all smashed.'

'Oh, Matt!' says Mum, and 'Sorry,' says Dad, 'I should have checked.'

Bronwyn is turning green. Mum grabs her quickly and drags her out to the corridor. 'It's a bit hot in there,' she calls.

But I can hear Bronny wailing, 'I couldn't even tell it was Anna!'

Dad asks quickly if I've seen the doctor. I describe the ward round. Dad erupts—my placid father, incandescent in white rage—'Tell this cowboy . . . '

Matt pipes up, 'Are there cowboys in hospital?'

'No,' I say, and thank God, it's time for Dad to take them to school. Mum will stay a little longer, all day if I like, but I know that's impossible, she'd have to close the nursery. I say I'd rather sleep. Dad asks if I know his work number—of course I don't, I never ring him at work. He hands over his card. *Peter Duncan, Chartered Accountant,* will come as soon as I need him, cancel appointments to be here in a moment.

Come on, God, what have I done to deserve this? If you want to kill me, do it quickly. Punch my teeth out one by one; pry my fingernails off with rusty nails, anything but this, this has gone right off the borders of pain and into another galaxy. I can't take it!

Painkillers bring me back to earth. I'm propped up in bed on an arrangement of pillows when Hayden appears, looking even taller than usual, broad shoulders and big hands awkward in this sterile environment. I feel breathless at the sight of him; my hands are shaky, my heart pounding. I've never felt this way about anyone before.

He's brought me a bunch of white carnations. 'They're not much, compared to all those.' He gestures to the perfect cellophane-covered arrangements which have poured in during the day: from the school, the karate club, Aunt Jackie in Perth, Oma and Opa in Holland. 'I didn't know if you'd even want to talk to me.'

'It wasn't your fault. And everyone says I'll be right in a couple of weeks; it's no big deal.'

'You weren't there,' he says, illogically but truly, and corrects himself, 'you don't know what it was like—I can still hear you screaming. Then I thought you were dead. We jemmied the door off and tried to lift you out but you grabbed your neck and screamed again, and we stopped till the ambulance came.'

I try to remember, but it's someone else's story; no memory surfaces.

Dad comes in early next morning to catch the ward round; he wants to know whether I should be transferred to a Melbourne hospital, for specialised care.

Mr Osman, the great orthopaedic god, is not impressed. 'Yarralong District Hospital,' he snaps condescendingly, 'is well equipped to deal with your daughter's injuries.' He goes on to explain the plan for the day: my thumb needs an operation—it's in eleven pieces; he's going to try to screw it together.

I don't want a general anaesthetic; I've seen 'GP' and documentaries; I know it will hurt my neck. I don't think I'll live if the pain gets worse. He promises an 'arm block' and Dad signs the consent forms; I feel so old, but I'm not old enough to sign my own name.

A few hours later the anaesthetist pumps me full of Valium till I'm floating and witty—except that my brain's lost contact with my body, so my mouth doesn't work.

Alex, the young doctor, returns in the afternoon, when everything's reconnected itself. (He's gorgeous; I've just noticed. This is not how I want to meet gorgeous men.) The operation is a success; the long bone of my thumb has been screwed neatly back together again. 'You'll make metal detectors scream.'

I smile because he is; I'm not sure how I feel about being a walking alarm bell.

'But the joint at the base of your thumb ... I'm afraid it's in *twelve* pieces now. It was pretty well smashed.'

Success must mean the whole thing didn't drop off.

Matt is wearing jeans, Bronwyn's check blouse, and Mum's straw gardening hat.

'He's a cowboy,' Mum explains.

This must be a mistake; life isn't supposed to be like this. Pain's supposed to be nasty but bearable, like period pain or cracking a rib. Nobody tells you that real pain is more than something in your body, it's a black vortex that engulfs your mind, leaving you wondering if there's a border between life and death and which side you're on. It leaves you knowing you're not the person you always thought you were, knowing you're not strong or brave, not even a person, just a speck in the maelstrom.

'I never thought I'd see this—Anna Duncan sitting still!'

'Haven't you got the nurses organised into aerobics yet?'

Jenny, Caroline and I have been together since the first day of Year 7, though we're all so different we sometimes wonder why. Neither of them cares about sport, and I live for it; on everything else they're the two extremes—even physically, though they're both shorter than me. Jenny's bubbly, warm, disorganised, with mousy-brown fluffy hair—rounder than she wants to be, but guys find her very attractive. Caroline's sharp, clever and petite, with very dark, very glossy neat hair, fastidious about her appearance and everything she puts in or on her body, and ultra-organised—we foresee a great career in computers for her.

Jenny rushes in to see me right after school, still in checked dress and white socks, not bothering to go home to change. Caroline comes later, looking cool and perfect and bringing little presents, flowers or talc or strawberries.

It's the best part of the day, the Jenny then Caroline time.

Morning pans are late again. Ruby rings first, then Mrs Hogan, then me. 'Try all together,' Mrs Hogan suggests, but that doesn't work either. Nurses bustle by in the corridors: 'We can't last forever!' Ruby calls after their disappearing, starched blue backs.

Tablet Sister, busy sisters, the man cleaning the floors— 'Don't jolt the bed!' Ruby orders. 'I won't be responsible for what happens.'

Breakfast comes and goes; more nurses pass.

'Wish I was a man,' Mrs Hogan moans. 'Chuck out the flowers and use a vase.'

I eye my flowers; decide it wouldn't work; punch my bell again. Ruby shouts. Mrs Hogan looks desperate and warns Ruby not to make her laugh. The body in the corner groans; the blankets shift and an unmistakable stench seeps out.

Footsteps in the hall. We won't let this one get past.

'Tea, ladies? Cold drink?'

Poor man. It's not his fault we're hysterical, two old women and a girl, helpless as—not babies, babies have nappies, at least—helpless as a patient in a hospital bed.

'Sorry, Sister!' says Ruby, from behind her curtain.

'That's all right,' says Busy Butt, grater-voiced, wiping her shoe. 'Just let me manage the pan next time.'

'You're a wicked old woman!' says Mrs Hogan, as the affronted back disappears.

'This is war,' claims Ruby, 'and it's the only weapon we've got.'

A guy in a St Pat's blazer is heading towards my bed; I didn't think I knew anyone there except Hayden. This is his friend Mark. He's brought me a big box of chocolates and the news that Hayden's been wagging school all week.

'He's really cut up about this,' Mark says, and I go through my lines again: it wasn't Hayden's fault; there wasn't anything he could have done.

'That's what I've been telling him—he says the other guy slowed down at the Give Way sign, as if he was going to stop, and then speeded up when you got there.'

That's as far as I can remember—the car, fast and white in a cloud of dust, swooping up the road on our left, Hayden braking, then—'It's okay, he's seen us'—and then the terror. Suddenly I'm chilled and trembly. 'It was as if he was trying to trick us! There was no way Hayden could have worked that out—tell him to stop feeling guilty.'

'I'll try. But it's not easy . . . you know he's crazy about you?'

'Really?' *So it wasn't just the excitement of the tournament!*

He grins. 'Let's say he's mentioned you a few times. And I heard all about Melbourne—he said you cleaned up.'

'I'm not so good at kata—that's the formal routine—a bit slow and boring. But I went pretty well in the fighting.'

'He'll have to watch it when you get out of here.'

This is the best present I've had so far: something to look forward to.

Hospital time is different from real time; there are days and nights, visitors and darkness, toast for breakfast and salad for lunch, but the only real marker is tablet time. Every four hours the white pills come. I don't want to know what they are; I don't care that I don't believe in drugs—I take them and the cycle begins: swallow, wait and anticipate . . . pain deadened just enough for me to start remembering who I am and catch the stray thoughts that wander into my head . . . then pain nagging, attention-seeking . . . and pain victorious again, re-energised for an endless fourth hour, as long as a month of maths, before the time's up and the tablet nurse can come around again.

If days only last for four hours, no wonder I've been here for so long. A month, maybe two. Caroline tells me they've made it through the first week of Year 12, but I think she's counted wrong. School was going to start the day after the tournament, and that was infinitely more than a week ago.

Ward round again, and Mr Osman stops at my bed.

'Whiplash should have healed by now. We'll do a CT scan to double check.'

I'm so surprised at God speaking directly to me that he's nearly out of the room before I ask what a CT scan is.

Like a better X-ray. It will give a clear picture of my vertebrae.

'So you think I *have* broken my neck?'

'It's probably better news if you have,' he explains breezily. 'This much pain from whiplash could mean long-term problems, but if it's a broken bone it will heal up quite quickly.'

One o'clock comes, and the X-ray porter with it. He's a fat, balding man of sixty, but so gentle as he helps me into a wheelchair, down halls and lifts, and finally onto a narrow bed at the mouth of a gleaming metal tunnel, that I'm ready to fall in love with him.

In the womb of the scanner I lie very still. Lights flash and spin, the machine whirrs, and I do my karate meditation until I fall asleep.

'I've never heard of that before,' the porter says. 'No one ever goes to sleep in there!'

I sleep again till Alex arrives with the good news of the scan. He looks as if he's going to cry as he tries to convince us both that a hangman's fracture, an unstable fractured C2, a broken neck, is something to celebrate. He explains the pictures; I understand nothing except the white line of destruction across the ring of bone.

'So why aren't I paralysed?'

'Because it was the bone that snapped; not the spinal cord. If it had been the cord, you wouldn't have been worrying about paralysis . . .'

That's a relief.

'. . . you'd be dead.'

He locks me into a strong metal frame to hold my heavy head. 'You can take it off in bed,' he says. 'But if you want to roll over you must have two nurses. For medico-legal reasons.'

What the hell are medico-legal reasons? Does he mean in case I *die*? Does it even matter if I die, or just if my parents sue?

Jenny rushes in; stops and turns pale at the sight of my scaffolded neck. Every day I've been telling her that I'll be better soon; back at school in a couple of weeks—as if the more I repeated it, the faster it would come true. But not today. This isn't what she expected to see—and for a moment Jenny, sunny, effervescent, ever-optimistic Jenny, stares at me and can't speak.

'They made a mistake—I broke my neck after all.'

Jenny begins to cry. And I think that maybe this is what best friends are for, not to be brave for you, but to tell you this is real, and it stinks.

But Jenny is Jenny. She stops herself quickly and is busy trying to think of all the reasons why life is better with a broken neck, when Mum arrives. Jenny turns to her and begins again: the frame's not so bad, is it, once you get used to it, and she thought that people died of a broken neck, and isn't Anna lucky—aren't we all lucky—that she didn't.

If Jenny had turned pale, Mum turns white and actually staggers once before dropping into the armchair by my bed.

'What do you mean, "broke her neck?" You've got whiplash, that's all; that's what the doctor said: *whiplash!*'

'They changed their minds.'

Jenny tennis-watches, from me to Mum and back again, and quickly decides it's time to leave.

'How could they not have known?' Mum demands, her voice rising, accent thickening. 'All this time! And then they don't even bother to ring me—just leave you here alone with it!'

And suddenly I can't be bothered with the crap about it being good news, better than whiplash and so on. The brave front is washed away in a tidal wave of rage and despair—my whole body knows this is the worst news it's ever heard. 'It's so unfair! Why did all this happen to me—and the man who hit us didn't get *anything*? Why couldn't *he* have died instead of me?'

I hear the words as they escape, sharp as flying glass; cutting away the last of the colour in Mum's face. She rubs away tears with the back of her hand. 'Jenny's right,' she says at last. 'We're so lucky you didn't. No matter what happens— I'm so glad to have my daughter.'

'Bollocks!'

It's the middle of the night. The voice is clear and distinct, not Ruby's or Mrs Hogan's. 'Bollocks!'

I've gone mad instead of dead.

I will myself back to sleep.

That's the end to lounging in bed propped on pillows; for the next six weeks I'll either be securely locked in my frame or lying straight and flat on a board-hard bed.

Lying flat is being trapped like a rabbit in a snare. *Does the rabbit know it's going to die? Does it thrash legs and ears in its last desperate fight against immobility and death? I'll die if I fight. It's the same thing.*

In my frame I'm freer. I fight the exhaustion as long as I can, sitting up in my cage till the pain makes me beg for mercy and rest. It's still the first full day, though; I have to give in right after lunch, and am nearly asleep when I hear Ruby say, 'Go on—she'll want to see you.'

Hayden. Wagging again. The grapevine told him this morning; he'd been sure it was wrong, a crazy grape of a lie, but hadn't been able to rest till he knew.

'It doesn't hurt more because I know it's broken—and the spasms are way better with the frame on.'

Maybe it wasn't the right moment to admit to muscle spasms. He slumps into the chair beside me, where I can't see him.

'You won't be able to do your black belt,' he says, hiding his face on the sheet; on my chest. 'I won't do my grading either.'

A flood of emotion surprises me, and I stroke his hair. He has thick, brown, wavy hair, very nice to touch.

'If you don't do it either,' I say, 'that bastard's beaten us. There'll be another grading in eight months—get your last brown belt stripe now, and we'll do our black belts together.' The feel of his breathing, warm against my breast, is melting me with tenderness.

'I want to kill him,' Hayden says. His voice is shaking and if I could see his eyes there would be tears. 'I keep on dreaming about it; I'm so afraid that if I see him I'll do it.'

He moves his face against the sheet, drying his eyes and rubbing against my nipple on the way. He flushes and jerks away from the bed. 'Anna, I didn't mean—'

'I know,' I say, and wish he'd kiss me.

'How come you didn't die?' Matt asks.

'Just lucky, I guess.'

'Will you die now?'

'Matthew!' groans Dad.

'Not if I can help it!'

'If you died, Bronny would be the oldest. Would I still be the youngest?'

There are two Annas. One joins in the chatter and surface of daily life, of being a friend, a daughter, a patient; this Anna knows that if you're strong and cheerful and fight fair you win the game and live happily ever after. That's the rule and she plays by the rule because that's the only way she knows how to fight—if you drop the rules the game is chaos, a street fight where you don't know who your opponents are.

The other Anna has no shape or role. She is an amorphous blob who just *is*. She is a black hole of pain and misery and terror, sucking the rays of friendship and politeness into oblivion. She floats above and around and behind the cheerful Anna, threatening to obliterate and swallow her down into that nothingness. And sometimes I think that she's the real me, but that can't be true, I won't let her, I've been the first Anna for so long, it's the only way I know how to be me.

It's morning tea time. The anaesthetist, masked and gowned, runs into my room. 'Anna,' she cries, 'I just heard! Thank God you didn't have a general anaesthetic!'

She runs out again.

'Why?' I ask Tablet Sister.

'They have to move your head a bit for a general—I guess it could have damaged the cord.'

Three times lucky. Three times my fragile spinal cord, no longer protected by its ring of bone, could have snapped and didn't.

When the car hit and my neck jerked so hard it broke.

When I screamed and stopped my rescuers from pulling me out of the car.

And then when I had the arm block instead of a general anaesthetic.

I *hate* my frame and bedpans and nurses washing me and everything about being in hospital. But they're better than the alternative.

(HAPTER 3

Pain is an animal, a shark, a crocodile, devouring me, crunching ravaged mouthfuls of my flesh. Pain is a noise, a siren's scream exploding through my body.

Mum wants to take some time off so she can be home with me when I leave here. (*If* I leave; the time has stretched so long already that sometimes I can't imagine living anywhere except this bed between Ruby and Mrs Hogan.) She's nearly crying as she tells me that Chris, who does weekends and the odd extra days, has just taken a full-time job in a pharmacy.

'She'll be able to give you things for sick plants.' (A dumb joke—but Mum standing by my bed sobbing is more than I can take.)

'I'll just close it.'

'Don't be silly, Mum! You've only just got it going—you can't close it now! I'll be okay on my own.'

'You won't,' says Dad. 'Not for a while. But with a million unemployed across the country, we should be able to find someone.'

'Do you want to see a social worker?' Alex asks. 'You've had a considerable trauma—it might be useful to talk to someone.'

But I can't see the point—pain goes away faster if you ignore it; no point sitting around thinking about it.

'It still mightn't be a bad idea,' Mum says when I tell her. 'You've had an emotional shock too, not just physical.'

'I may have broken bones, Mum, but there's nothing wrong with my mind!'

Ruby's been waiting all day for 'Sun and Surf'. By eight o'clock I realise she's not joking. It really is her favourite program.

The plot's fairly basic: Bronzed Hunk meets Big Boobs. One tries to drown, the other rescues. A bit of lust in the sand, action shots of surf and sea, boobs and rippling pecs everywhere.

Ruby is old enough to be the oldest hunk's grandmother—but she's obviously not thinking about knitting booties now.

'You know the worst thing about getting old?' she asks, when the last romantic clinch has faded from the screen and our lights are out. 'It's knowing that you've missed your chance at all those things you've never done.'

'You could always buy boobs like hers.'

'Maybe I'll do that. Tell the doctor to slip them on when he's doing the new hip.'

'And if you fall over,' Mrs Hogan points out, 'you'll bounce right back without hurting yourself.'

Ruby laughs. 'I still reckon I've missed my chances for rolling around on a beach with a handsome bloke.'

'You never know . . . there's life in the old girl yet. There might be someone out there waiting to meet you.'

'And little piggies might fly. Face it, Iris, I'm not going to meet Sean Connery now . . . Are you paying attention, young Anna? You've got that lovely boy; you get out of here and do whatever you want to. No point in lying in a lonely bed in sixty years time, wondering what it would have been like.'

'Stop corrupting the poor girl! You go to sleep, Anna, and don't listen to us wicked old women . . . Tell you what, Ruby, I'll lend you my husband.'

'Does he look like Sean Connery?'

'Close your eyes and you'd never know the difference.'

Last summer Caroline, Jenny and I deep-and-meaningfulled for most of one long night, wondering about everyone we know—who's still a virgin and who's not. Most of our friends are, we're pretty sure. Unfortunately, since none of us had a boyfriend at the moment, we couldn't decide on the really crucial question: which of the three of us would be first? But I never thought I'd be having a slumber party with eighty-year-olds and talking about the same thing.

It's not exactly a nightmare; there are no pictures, no story. Only feeling.

I'm sinking in woolly blackness, thick, choking blackness. I want to claw my way out but can't move, want to scream but don't know how. A strangled squeak. Another and another. Not loud enough to wake my roommates or bring scurrying nurses—but, finally, enough to wake me.

I'm alive, I'm okay. *But with the choking terror still stuck fast in my throat and my heart pounding so fast and hard it hurts, the blackness is more real than my bed.*

Student nurse Fiona is back.

'You know how you had your accident on the corner of Woolshed Road and the highway?'

I know.

'We live down Woolshed Road, and people were ringing my mum all the next day, because they heard a girl had been hurt, and they thought it was me!'

'Wasn't it lucky it was me.'

I picture all those worried-about-Fiona people, queuing for a telephone, overcome with joy because thank God, it was only Anna Duncan. Fiona, lucky Fiona, was still bouncy and healthy and on the right side of a hospital bed.

Now she's telling me about the man who hit us. She uses his name, Trevor Jones—I hadn't thought of him as a person with a name like anyone else—and suddenly I'm swamped by shock, drowning in a flood of pure, burning hatred.

Fiona, with the sensitivity of a bulldozer in a rainforest, chatters on. He's her brother's best mate, a really good bloke.

That's supposed to make me feel better? But the waves of hate are still crashing over me—if I open my mouth, I'll choke.

'He's really upset, couldn't even drive for a couple of days afterwards.'

'I couldn't either!'

She gives me a funny look and wanders off.

Jenny of course has told her mum who's told her best friend who happens to be a faith healer and has turned up here to heal me. Would I mind if she prays for me?

How do I say no? She sits beside me, her hand on mine. She asks the Virgin Mary, Jesus and all 'my loved ones who have gone before' to intervene for me, and begins to pray. *This is so embarrassing, what if someone else comes in?* It's a long prayer, detailing the parts of my body that need healing, all the way down to corpuscles and capillaries. Her voice is gentle and deep, hypnotic, maybe—and in spite of myself I'm dropping into a warm sea of peace, floating on a vast lap of blue; strong arms cradle me lovingly, rock me tenderly. The peace seeps through my bones and blood, melting pain, healing hurt, dissolving muscles and will so deeply I can barely move my lips to thank her at the final Amen. Lying still and quiet, my eyes brimming with tears, my soul overflows with the exquisite certainty that I'll be well soon, quickly and completely.

Half the class have come with Jenny and Caroline tonight: a swarm of friends—a blur of faces, a hum of voices. They'd wanted to surprise me, but I surprise them instead, and the sight of me quiets them in a way teachers would die for.

My head aches as I try to follow the ball of conversation; Chris to Caroline, Josh to Emma, Thula to Brad, Caroline back to Mia. Only Jenny sits quietly, watching me, deflecting answers as if she sees that I can't snatch the words as they flit through the air, but it's more than that, the noise is building inside my brain—I can't tell who's speaking; the words are garbled like an untuned channel.

Busy Butt bustles in. Two visitors at a time, she says. A couple of you stay, the rest out to the hall, wait your turn or come back another day.

I groan with the rest, make faces behind her departing wobbly bum, and silently thank God for rules.

Jenny and Caroline stay; the others disappear. They'll come back another day in pairs, they say.

I don't mention to anyone that I had trouble understanding the conversation. Not Jenny or Caroline, or my mum or the doctor. It doesn't seem important. And at the back of my mind, I think that if it is important, I don't want to know.

Six weeks in this frame, Osman said, and four more in a foam collar, add a couple of months to get back into training after that . . . no matter how hard I work, I'm not going to make the state team this year. Winning one tournament doesn't take the place of the trials. I'll never be the under-eighteen title holder myself. *Never . . . impossible . . . too late—how can a dream be killed like that? Glowing within reach one minute, ripped out of me and out of sight the next.*

Aunt Lynda, my father's sister, is a nurse in Melbourne; she loves shocking us with gross, funny stories about hospital life. Italian and Greek women aren't popular in hospitals, she claims. They cry too much and upset the ward routines. (She laughs when Mum calls herself a clog wog, and says they're okay, just as buttoned-up as Anglo-Saxons.) But I'm crying this morning, secretly and silently as a kid at school camp—and am caught by a nurse on early rounds. Is it the pain, he asks.

'No; I'm okay.' *Leave me alone.*

'Are you *sure* you're not in pain?'

'I want to go back to school.' Not quite the truth, but as near as I can get it.

'Wish my kids would say that! All I can do to get them off some mornings.'

So I behave; I'm not going to be caught again. And the tears are bubbling so viciously now they'll drown me if I let them go—shove them back below the surface; if I wait long enough maybe they'll evaporate.

I wonder if I would have been re-X-rayed if I'd been Italian. It's something to think about, in the long white nights, when I'm afraid to move in my unsafe bed. For medico-legal reasons.

'I've got a sore throat,' Bronwyn announces, in case I hadn't noticed the subtle stink of VapoRub. 'Mum says I don't have to go to school.'

Mum gives her a quick hug. 'You're coming to work with me, aren't you? A couple of days off and you'll be fine.'

'Better not put her near your "scented garden" section,' I tease. 'She'll put the customers right off.'

Jenny, reassured that I'm going to live, quizzes me on more important matters. 'You really like Hayden? Really, *really* like?'

I really, *really* like him. My stomach churns at his name; my head floats at the sight of him. Even the sound of his voice leaves me breathless.

'Sounds like love to me,' Jenny agrees, nodding wisely. 'But it's funny. You sort of liked him before—but you weren't crazy about him. And now ... you get all these injuries and the other driver and Hayden get nothing! I know he didn't do anything wrong, but I think I'd still blame him, if it were me.'

Safe in my new cage, I'm allowed to move—wheeled ignominiously across the hall on a rolling toilet seat—but anything's better than bedpans. And a bath! Oh God, to be clean at last. Because that special BO of pain and sweat, never properly wiped away with a damp washer and deodorant, is strong enough to knock out a football change room. No wonder Hayden didn't kiss me.

Busy Butt strips me, slides me onto another chair with its own personal crane, cranks it up and lowers me into the tub. (Does anyone get used to just how *weird* hospital is? Would it be easier if you joined a nudist colony first?)

'Don't get the frame wet,' she says. 'The padding might come unstuck.'

Oh well, I didn't want to wash the top half anyway. At least I'll have nice clean legs—if I can see them through the regrowth.

'How about I shave them for you?' she offers.

Feels strange. Strange but nice.

And now Alex, gorgeous dark-eyed Alex, so kind—and so disappointingly unaware that I'm female he must be gay—is kneeling before me, swaddling my right foot in bandages and plaster.

'I'll put a heel on it,' he says. 'You'll be able to walk when it's dry.'

But I need a lesson first, in case I've forgotten how to walk in the last two weeks.

'We'll give you a sling,' the physio says, 'to keep that thumb out of the way. You couldn't use crutches anyway.'

Thank God for that! My head in a cage, my arm in a sling and foot in plaster . . . that's about enough.

We head off down the hall. It doesn't feel natural; I'm light-headed and wobbly, hugging the walls for safety, step after tentative step. But I'm walking; I'm getting better.

And I'm glad to get back to my room!

'Well done,' says Mrs Hogan. 'You'll be up and about in no time.'

Ruby dissolves into giggles. 'You look like a robot!'

'Can you dance like the man on TV now?' Matt asks.

'You know,' Bronwyn adds hopefully, while Matt demonstrates, 'the one with a plaster on his foot and crutches.'

I remember the ad, but skip the dancing. Their faces fall—'But you can sign my cast!'—and they cheer up again. Matt draws a fat cat and a misshapen dog; Sally and Ben, waiting for me to come home.

Ruby's got one new hip and is waiting for a second; Mrs Hogan's got a new knee ... why couldn't I have a new neck?

'Or put us all together and you'd get one good person!'

'There aren't that many bits of me you'd want!'

'Your pretty young face,' Mrs Hogan says kindly.

Mrs Hogan lied.

It's the first time I've been allowed to walk to the toilet. It's the first time I've stood to wash my hands in the sink and seen the mirror above it.

It can't be a mirror—it's a sick joke, someone's painted a face from a haunted house onto the glass! That back-from-the-dead scarecrow woman can't *be me!* The face is grey and gaunt, the cheekbones sharp. The hair is so greasy it's almost grey too. The only colour comes from the angry red scars below the mouth and left eye.

I can see that Alex might not be gay. I can see even more why Hayden didn't kiss me.

Jenny's unlucky enough to be the next visitor. 'Why didn't you tell me I looked like a witch?'

She laughs and says it's not that bad, I just look like I'm not feeling the best. Nice try. It doesn't convince me.

But Jenny has more important news. She's in love.

'Do you remember the new guy, the morning we picked up our books?'

Vaguely. Might be easier if I'd made it to school for a day.

'Costa. Costa Mavronas.' The name says it all. At least the way she says it.

'Let me guess. He's gorgeous?'

'Unbelievable!'

'I must be sicker than I thought. A gorgeous guy in the same room and I didn't notice?'

'Actually I didn't either at first. Not till I talked to him. It's his eyes; they're ... '

'Brown?'

She doesn't even realise that I'm taking the mickey. She actually shivers! This is serious; I've never seen her like it before. 'They're incredible. You have to meet him!'

'Jenny, I don't care how good friends we are—there's no way I'm meeting a gorgeous guy while I look like this. Not even the love of your life.'

If I give in to the pain, will the blackness suck me in? If I give in to the blackness, will the pain let me go?

I can't do much about the rest of me, but this hair is unbearable. I've got to wash it.

Maria says she'll do it. She lies me flat in my foam collar, my head at the foot of the bed. I hope she knows what she's doing: it'd be stupid to die for the sake of clean hair. But it's *so* dirty!

Maria is tiny and wiry with a faint moustache; she's a nurse's aid, not a sister. She washes my hair carefully, almost lovingly; dries it gently and styles with mousse and pride. I feel clean, new and fresh; for at least an hour I feel like a human being.

Are there any new humiliations left? My period's early—and torrential. Blood floods onto the sheets, the floor, the shower; onto my new plaster cast. Ingenious Maria draws pictures with fat black texta, a house with a long path and flowers, to disguise the blood.

My mother told me once about her friend whose child had died. Standing there by his empty bed, she began to bleed, out of control, as if her body had opened to pour out grief. Can a uterus understand the death of a child, a child it nourished patiently, from seed to fish to babe? How could it not?

My mind flits from one disaster story to another, searching for meaning.

It's nearly time for my friends to come after school. I get what I need from my drawer and ask Busy Butt to take me to the toilet. She walks me across the hall and leaves me in privacy.

And doesn't return. I ring the bell, ring it again . . . go on waiting. The price of privacy.

When the door does finally open, it's still not a nurse. It's Caroline—Ruby's decided that I'm stranded and has sent her to collect me. As I wash my hands she says, 'Oh, Anna!'; wets a paper towel and dabs at my legs, at the unnoticed, unreachable trickle of blood.

If I say anything I'll cry. I'm too embarrassed to be grateful.

'That's what friends are for,' she says.

I don't know if I believe in you, God, but I'm so angry now that I'd rather think there was something there to hate. So angry: if you were here I'd spit in your face and tell you how I felt. You're a fraud—you trick people into worshipping you, you and your mercy are nothing but lies. I don't know what you think I did to deserve this, but I will never forgive you and never, never, stop hating you.

'A woman like that! Haunches on her like a working bullock!'

It's the middle of the night; the 'bollocks!' voice again. It hasn't woken anyone else. Maybe I dreamt it.

The bed in the corner creaks as the old woman tosses and mutters.

The nurses hate my frame, the nail-breaking clips, the responsibility of the wobbling head before it's braced; the nuisance of finding two nurses to do it at once. A new nurse is on this morning; she's done it before, nothing to it; she doesn't need a helper.

She whacks me across the neck with a red-hot branding iron.

I scream.

'Behave yourself!' she snaps. 'It barely touched you!'

She does up the final clip with a jerk to let me know who's boss.

The world turns black; I can't see. As it comes back I explode. Scream, shout, swear. Rage like this and I could spar with van Damme.

Tablet Sister comes in to see what the trouble is.

'I've bloody broken my neck!' I shout. 'Don't tell me it doesn't hurt!'

Ruby and Mrs Hogan begin to clap.

Apart from those mysterious midnight outbursts, the old woman in the corner hasn't woken since I've been here. Her son comes at lunchtime to spoon soup and custard into her mouth; she won't eat much for the nurses. If that's a choice, it's the only sign of life she gives. The last few nights I've woken to hear the nurses, clucking quietly, working by torchlight to wash her and change her sheets.

But tonight the sounds are different. There are no suppressed giggles or the occasional 'Oh, yuck!' that makes me try not to picture what they're cleaning. Curtains are pulled—

mine, Ruby's and Mrs Hogan's—then whispered commands and the sound of wheels. When I wake again in the morning her bed is gone—and so is Mrs McPherson. I didn't even know her name till she died.

Shouldn't I be just a little bit shocked ... sad ... *something*?

It'd be cold enough not to feel anything, but what I feel is worse—a superstitious feeling, as if death really is a Grim Reaper, out hunting to fill his quota for the night. What I feel is relief that he found the right person.

Plus a bit of frustration. Now I'll never find out about the woman with haunches like a working bullock.

Mum's found someone to work in the nursery. A friend's son who's just quit uni after two years of business studies; said it wasn't what he wanted out of life and came home to sort out what was.

Dad's not impressed. He wonders what had to be sorted out and why. And if Mum thinks that two years of business studies would actually make any difference to running a nursery, she'd better think again.

'Luke's okay,' says Mum. 'He's keen to work, and he's interested in plants.'

Dad snorts. 'You'd better check what kind.'

Dad's been so cranky since I've been here! It's not like him—Mr Conservative Accountant, maybe, but usually pretty tolerant underneath.

Valentine's Day. Hayden comes in after school and hands me a card. Not too mushy, just 'To my Valentine' with a picture of red roses—and inside, 'Love, Hayden.' Love. He stares out the window while I read it. He looks like a little boy when he's embarrassed. If I could reach I'd hug him.

'Thanks,' I say instead. 'It's nice.'

'When you get out of here . . . when you're a bit better . . . do you want to go out?'

'That'd be great.' *Now kiss me, go on!* No; no such luck. But he mustn't think I'm completely hideous if he wants to go out.

'There's a present too,' and out of his school bag—better than red roses—comes my trophy. A replacement, he explains; the Association has sent it up, via the club, via Hayden.

'The one you had was smashed,' he says. 'That must be how you wrecked your thumb.'

It stands proudly on my bedside table, gold among the flowers.

'I'd hate to see the guy that lost,' says the tea man.

I'm going home. In a wheelchair, with a neck brace, plaster, sling and occupational therapist Julie and only for a visit—but if I pass today, tomorrow I'll be home for good.

February air is hotter than I'd remembered; in the air-conditioned hospital I cover myself with blankets to stop the shivering, and the nurses wear cardigans. A smell of dust and roses wafts across the carpark; the world is bright and large, as if I've taken sunglasses off. (Was I wearing my sunnies? It was a hot, clear day, a little after four . . . Guess I'll need new ones.)

Julie drives slowly, with exaggerated care over the railway track and speed bumps, but I'm too excited to mind a bit more pain. A white car coming up on our left makes me hold my breath, but I'm not as nervous as I was afraid I might be. My dad's favourite saying: 'Nothing so frightening as fear itself.' But I'm okay. Six months and I'll be eighteen, with a licence and independence. One accident isn't going to change my life.

Dad's waiting in the driveway, looking a bit anxious and tired. I'd never realised he had so much grey in his hair—the worries of looking after other people's money. *It can't be about me, can it, this grey hair and crankiness?*

He helps the OT lift the wheelchair out.

No, I say, let me walk.

Dad looks doubtful; Julie says please, she's responsible for my safety—and the path, rock slabs overgrown with thyme, is rough and narrow. I have to give in—'But I won't use it inside!'

Dad pushes me to the door, doing his best to avoid the bumps, yanking a piece of lavender out of the spokes and over the back fence as if it's to blame for everything from car accidents to world recession.

The heavy scent fills the air. Julie breathes in deeply, gazing out over the rockery and knot garden, down to the wattles shielding the river on the far side of the fence, 'It's a beautiful place.' I explain about my mother's herb nursery, grown from hobby to passion to business.

We reach the steps. One, two, three and I've made it, Dad and Julie hovering on either side. The lounge room, left untidy in the early morning rush, still looks fresh and new, bigger somehow, and welcoming. I'm ready to sit down.

The couch is too low. So are the chairs. I try to bend and it doesn't work.

'It's okay,' Julie says. 'You can still go home! We'll lend you a high armchair.'

With that—as well as a shower chair, a shower hose and non-slip mat, a raised toilet frame, a long-handled reacher, a bed cradle to keep the blankets off my sore feet, an angled bookboard so that I can read and write, and of course the wheelchair—I pass.

Tomorrow I can go home and stay home.

Mum arrives at the hospital right after breakfast. After she's packed she has a lesson in putting my frame on and taking it off; in sitting me up and lying me down.

I say goodbye to the new patient in Mrs Hogan's bed, wish Ruby all the best and leave her some of my flowers.

Mum signs me out, we're given tablets and an appointment card to see Mr Osman in a fortnight. Tablet Sister and Busy

Butt wish me luck—and for a few moments I feel quite weepy, as if I'm leaving behind some significant part of my life. Maybe I am.

Finally I'm home. Mum and I celebrate with a cup of coffee and a chocolate cake; her face starts to relax. She's as glad to have me back as I am to be here. The house glows with peace, and quiet.

Mum puts me to bed for a nap; I could almost ask for my teddy. In my own bed, in my own room, I sleep for three hours.

CHAPTER 4

'How come you've still got that thing on? I thought you'd be all better!'

'Matt, you're so *stupid*! We're supposed to be nice to Anna!'

'And how come they let you bring all those flowers home?'

'Because they're *her* flowers, idiot!'

'Bronwyn, stop calling your brother stupid!'

Mum harassed, kids fighting—now I know I'm home.

'Can I have some in my room too?'

'Me too?'

'Okay—just not the carnations.' But they're not interested in Hayden's plain white flowers, they want the biggest, the brightest; the extra ribbons and bows. They choose and change, tearing from mantelpiece from windowsill—with a weird kind of slow-motion tiptoe past my chair—and whisk their prizes back to their own rooms.

Teatime now—feels like midnight—fried rice, my favourite. I drop my fork. It's barely hit the tiles before Matt and Bronny are out of their chairs and under the table, cracking heads in the race to pick it up.

'Relax, you two,' Dad tells them. 'You'll have lots of chances to help her.'

'I'm not going to need help for that long!'

I shouldn't have snapped. My first night home; everyone's trying so hard. Too hard.

You'd think it'd be easier having your mum undress you than a stranger. You'd be wrong. Mum's getting me ready for bed. I have a go at my shirt buttons but my good hand has the shakes; she has to do it all, shirt, shorts and knickers. She's as embarrassed as I am, drawing her breath in sharply as she strips off my shirt. Then it's nightie on, unclip the frame, slip on the collar, take off the frame, lie me down, hoist my legs in, and do up the nightgown once I'm safe on my back.

I don't know if I can do this. Matt's not the only one who thought I'd be better once I got home; part of me must still believe in magic and thought that getting out of hospital would be an Abracadabra. No drum roll or fireworks—just a tiny little miracle, that's all I wanted.

And I'm warning you, God, I still feel the same way— you're not going to cheat me again. I'm going to be better faster than anyone you've ever seen. Beating an injury is just a question of how determined you are, and I'm determined. Six months is plenty—I'm not turning eighteen like this. That's a threat, God, or a promise; take it however you like.

Trapped in the blackness again. Suffocating, choking; motionless struggles; screams that take forever to wake me. The lingering terror, my pulse hammering.

'Sleep well?'
   'Okay, thanks.'
   I'm sitting on the end of my bed, stark naked except for the frame; Mum's kneeling in front of me, trying to stick my fat foot through my knickers. Everyone else has gone to school and work.

   The mirror in my bedroom is full length. It's watched me practise karate; inspected me with new clothes and none. Sometimes I even liked what it saw—like the morning of the tournament, the day it happened. I'd been doing warm-ups in my underwear, my hair still loose from the shower: stretch and flex, swivel and kick, boot the butterflies right out of my stomach. I jumped and spun, and just for an instant I saw a stranger in the mirror, the sun touching her hair with gold, her body sexy and strong ...

'Spectacular,' Mum says, meeting my eyes in the mirror. So she wasn't embarrassed last night; just amazed.

My breasts are mottled yellow and black. Can you get gangrene in boobs? Not that there's much left to drop off— nearly as flat as when I was thirteen. I think the mirror needs a poster over it again.

The district nurse bounces in just as Mum and I are about to start our sandwiches, and doesn't seem to think it's bizarre to walk into a stranger's house at lunchtime and ask her to strip.

Does she ever get mixed up when she goes out to dinner, and rush her friends into the bathroom?

My scaffolding doesn't faze her. 'Just wrap you up like the Christmas turkey,' she says, covering every bit that's not me in cling wrap and garbage bags. She soaps, shampoos, conditions; the hot water runs luxuriously over my neck and shoulders. I won't complain again about stripping at lunchtime.

A knock on the front door. I'm alone in the lounge room doing thumb aerobics—wiggle, wiggle, up-down, up-down—it'll be fit even if nothing else is.

Another knock ... *I'm not going to the door looking like this* ... where *is* everyone? Damn! I'll have to do it—maybe it's Jen.

It's a guy. About twenty; not especially tall but lean and fit; arms and legs tanned under the T-shirt and shorts, brown feet in his sandals. Long dark hair pulled back in a ponytail, and a gold stud in one ear—Dad won't be crazy about this. It's Luke, Mum's reliever.

I wait for the usual shocked look, the eyes wandering to the ceiling, the floor, anywhere but me—but it doesn't happen. Luke looks straight at me as he introduces himself. 'Heard you've had a rough time,' he says.

'I've had better.'

'I just came to tell your mum how everything's going. I haven't killed any plants, even sold a couple . . . and I got her a great deal on a truckload of garden gnomes.'

'You're kidding!'

'Yeah.'

He's got a way of looking down when he smiles, with a grin that flashes in fast and is gone, then just his eyes checking to see if you got it (blue eyes; surprisingly blue for the dark hair). I can see why Mum likes him.

'Matt, I'll kill you if you don't stop bouncing my bed!'

I open my eyes. The bouncing stops. The little brat is nowhere to be seen. Close my eyes; try to go back to sleep; the rocking starts. He stops again as soon as I open my eyes and shout.

'Matt, I'm warning you—get out from under my bed!'

Mum, Dad and Bronwyn stream into my room—followed by a bleary-eyed Matt.

It's the noise in my ears that's rocking the bed. Open my eyes, and the room is still. Shut them, and I'm on a stormy sea. It'd be funny if I didn't feel so seasick.

'You didn't tell us you had ringing in your ears!' Mum accuses.

'It's only bad when everything's quiet. I didn't think it was important. Sorry, Matt.'

He climbs onto the bed beside me to get a look at my ear. 'I still can't see your earrings!'

'You explain that one, Anna,' Mum says. 'I'm going to make pancakes for breakfast.'

Dad heads back to bed and Mum to the kitchen. She baked a mountain of slices and biscuits yesterday; if she doesn't watch out she'll turn into a regular *Women's Weekly* mother. And we'll turn into a family of hippos.

There could be worse fates. I'm just squeezing the lemon over my third pancake when the phone rings.

'Guess who called last night?'

Only one person could have Jenny out of bed this early on a Saturday morning. 'Brad Pitt?'

'Costa, you idiot! We're going to a movie—tonight!'

'What's on?'

'Us, I hope!'

'Subtle, Jen. What about the movie?'

'Who cares? What am I going to wear? God, Anna, I wish you could come over and help me choose!'

A quick calculation: four steps to the front door, more at the back, a brother who'd stare and a mother who'd fuss—I don't think I could face it even if I could get there. 'Bring some of your gear over here to try; maybe you could borrow something of mine ... what about my new skirt?'

'If I lose a kilo an hour and borrow your legs.'

'You want them, they're yours!'

'Sorry, I forgot. Okay, great, I'll come over.'

She arrives an hour later with her backpack bulging, and spreads her clothes across the bed. She tries on my mini-skirt, the one we bought at the sales the week before the accident, the one she flattered me into, and even if I never have the nerve again it was fun to wear it once. Jenny calls herself Elephant Legs but that's a lie, the skirt doesn't look bad at all—but it comes to a choice between doing it up and breathing, and in the end breathing wins.

'What about my white top with your long skirt?'

The top's clingy, and Jenny's got a good shape to cling to; it's lower on her than on me. She looks gorgeous. Sexy.

'Is it okay?'

'He'll go crazy.'

'Wish you and Hayden could come too.'

'You'll probably figure out something to do without us. Just ring me tomorrow and tell me what it was.'

But when she phones she doesn't really have much to say at all. Quiet and dreamy, barely giggles. I thought love was supposed to be fun, but Jenny's been hit by a sledgehammer. 'I'll bring your top back Monday,' she says. 'I'll tell you all about it then. But it was a good night; the best.'

There are some things you don't need to share even with your best friend. So I ask about the movie—though she doesn't seem to remember much about the storyline; trying not to be jealous; trying not to wonder exactly what turns good into best and if there's some light-years-away future where Hayden and I will have a night like that.

We're in the lounge room with my whole family. Very intimate. Mum's made coffee and handed around a few of the eight dozen biscuits; Bronwyn and Vinita are twirling across the room in their pink ballet leotards, shrieking if anyone looks at them.

Matt wants to know if Hayden's car is fixed yet.

'There wasn't enough left to fix. We're getting a new one as soon as the insurance coughs up.'

'So where's your car now?' Matt demands.

'Actually it was my mum's car ... it's at the wreckers.'

'Can I go see it?'

'I think you can go play outside,' Dad decides, shooing him towards the door. 'Bronny, you too. Let Anna talk to her friend by herself.' Apparently he and Mum are going to play in the garden too.

Hayden picks up his coffee mug; puts it down without drinking any. 'Your parents are pretty cool—I didn't know if they'd want me hanging around.'

'They probably figure we can't get up to much at the moment.'

'They might be right.' The way he's looking at me is not romantic. I shouldn't have reminded him. 'Do you feel any better now you're home?'

'At least I can sleep! Showers are still weird though.' I tell him my theory about the district nurse stripping her friends when she drops in for coffee. He looks embarrassed, as if he's not quite sure whether or not I'm trying to be funny.

This is such an awful way to get to know each other! Driving to Melbourne for the tournament is the only time we've ever spent together outside the karate hall.

'So what's been happening at karate?'

'Thursday was classic—Sempi Ross was demonstrating a sweep kick—only problem was he swept so hard his other foot shot out from under him and he landed on his bum. Of course for anyone else the whole dojo would have cracked up—but you know Sempi Ross.'

'He wasn't happy?'

'Not much. We really paid for it. We were practising blocking a hit to the ribs; Josh and I were really going well—you know when you get a rhythm up, you know you're doing it right and it feels great . . . '

What I wouldn't give to feel that now!

'But he kept us going so long we totally lost it. In the end we were just taking turns punching each other in the guts. I thought I'd broken a rib.'

'That was bright. What did Sensai say?'

'You know: "Technique, boys, technique!"'

It's a good imitation. I laugh more than he did at my district nurse joke.

Dad's brandishing the remains of the grandiose flower arrangement Gran and Pop sent me.

'What are Anna's flowers doing on Ben's bed?'

'I wanted to make it nice for Ben, since you won't let him inside any more!'

Dad softens back into the happy family mode he's been working at so hard all weekend. 'You know Ben can't remember not to jump up. He'd really hurt Anna if he knocked her over right now.'

'He could learn not to!'

Matt still believes in Santa Claus, the tooth fairy and the intelligence of his dog.

As well as gossip and froth, Jenny and Caroline brought books to the hospital and tried to tell me what they'd done in class. But the hospital was too loud, too busy; the hard facts of chemistry and maths bounced off the smooth walls. A novel for English was easier to hide behind, but not much more went in.

Now that I'm home, I tell myself—and my parents—I'll start studying seriously. And I try very hard; I don't want to admit that even without the interruptions, I can't remember the characters' names so I have to keep checking who they all are—then I lose my place and can't be bothered going on.

Monday afternoon Mr Sandberg—chemistry and home room—comes to see me. 'Well, this *is* a pain in the neck!' (He's also the absolute cliche-and-corny-joke king. Even worse than my dad.)

I groan, Mum makes coffee, and Mr Sandberg gets serious. Since it doesn't look as if I'll be back at school very soon, he says, we need to apply for 'deferment of assessments' to later in the year. But as long as I cover all the dot points, I won't need to do every bit of mundane work. There shouldn't be any problem in catching up.

'Especially if you switch the subjects that are heavy on pracs to something more theoretical. What are you aiming for?'

'Phys ed. Phys ed teacher.'

He pulls a face. 'Trust you not to make it easy!'

'Couldn't I do the written requirements now and catch up on the physical in second semester?'

He thinks we should be able to work something out. But chemistry pracs are impossible. 'You could switch to psychology—you're lucky it's early enough in the year that we've got these options.'

I don't want to do psychology! Life's too short to waste on waffle and soul-searching—get out there and get on with it, that's my philosophy!

But I don't have much choice—chemistry goes; we fiddle and trim. 'What about a tutor?' Mum asks.

'Let's wait and see. You're bright, Anna—and I've always had the feeling you've never worked quite as hard as you could. In a terrible way this could even be good for you—sometimes it takes trauma to show us what we're capable of when we really pull out all the stops.'

Lucky again.

Being so lucky drives me crazy.

Even in Casualty they said it: lucky the cut didn't get my eye; lucky the poke on the chin didn't knock out my teeth; and of course, breaking my neck has left me so lucky lucky lucky that I should sing like a lotto ad.

Bronwyn still smells like a human vaporiser. Dad takes her to the doctor while Mr Sandberg's visiting Mum and me. She returns looking smug.

'*I* have to gargle with salt water!' She dumps a spoonful of salt into a glass and disappears to the bathroom. Martyred coughs and gurgles trickle down the hall.

'There's nothing wrong with her throat,' Dad says. 'The doctor thought this might convince her of it.'

Next morning Bronwyn heads off to school with a scarf wrapped around her neck. 'It makes my throat feel better,' she says.

I don't think I need my new psychology text to work this one out. But Bronwyn's my parents' problem; I've got enough of my own.

An hour later an officer from the insurance company arrives. ('Officer' is right. She looks like a sergeant in some war training comedy. Older than Mum; short and stocky, grey hair chopped short—and the hairiest legs I've ever seen. Also slightly less sense of humour than her briefcase.)

She starts to explain how the system works: long-term assessments, disability percentages, compensation for permanent damage ... What's it got to do with me? My stomach's in knots just listening to her.

'Why would I have assessments *two years* from now?'

Hairy Legs glares. Just my life, I'm not supposed to speak.

'In my experience,' she pronounces, a fat grey prophet of doom, 'it's best to face facts early. It's my duty to let you know rights and procedures under the Act.' She starts on the spiel again.

'What facts?'

Hairy Legs turns back to the front page of her manila folder. 'Closed head injury, fractured C2'—she gestures at guilty me, caught rednecked with frame, bandage and plaster—'it's not impossible that Anna will be left with some residual difficulties.'

'Mr Osman,' Mum says firmly, 'expects that Anna will be fully recovered in six months. And so do we. Just tell us what we need to know now.'

What we need is forms: multi forms, long and involved, in triplicate. She hands them straight to Mum. Some advantages in being too young to take control.

Insurance, apparently, will cover all my medical and rehabilitation expenses; pay for a tutor if I need one; provide someone to stay at home with me during the day so my mother can go back to her nursery.

A babysitter. Some nice kind person coming to look after poor little Anna! Inexplicable panic slaps me.

'I'm enjoying the time at home,' Mum puts in quickly, seeing my face.

'It's up to you what you want to accept,' Hairy Legs says. 'A lot of my clients feel they'd rather manage on their own than have too many strangers in their lives.'

Was that a truce? Mum thinks so; she puts the kettle on.

I'm less forgiving. I'm not Road Accident Client number 304; injured-person-with-problem; I'm just *me*. Can't she see that?

Or maybe the panic is just because I haven't had my afternoon rest. Cranky baby; put me to bed before I cry.

Mum thinks I need a treat too. She brings Sally in and puts her on the bed beside me. The cat sniffs suspiciously and promptly jumps off.

'You must still smell of hospital,' Mum apologises.

But Sally's just asserting her right to find her own nap places. As soon as Mum leaves she jumps back on and curls up in her normal place by my left shoulder. Unhygienic, maybe, but comforting.

CHAPTER 5

Caroline, Jenny and I: 'The Three Amigos,' Dad teases, waiting for the groan—all part of the ritual.

I can almost believe that life is normal again, gossiping with my two best friends. Apparently the rest of the world didn't stop on the twenty-ninth of January—people are getting on with their lives, and one day I'll rejoin them. Meanwhile there's a lot to catch up on!

Mia's claimed the Canadian exchange student, who's a real spunk but goes feral if anyone thinks he's American. 'So of course Brad calls him a Yank whenever things are getting boring!'

'And Mrs Moore quit last Friday—three weeks into the term and she just walked out!'

'Why?'

'The school's not saying. It's all a bit weird.'

'She must have had a nervous breakdown.'

'After three weeks? Year 7s can't be that bad.'

Mum interrupts to bring us a jug of juice and biscuits. 'You're not getting tired, Anna?' she asks, but I don't *mind* being tired, don't mind being not quite able to follow the banter, it's just so good to sit here and listen to it.

We settle down with our drinks and Jenny picks up where she left off, which is how extra unbearable Chris has been since she was elected school captain.

The juice is quivering in my glass, the shaking worse with holding it so long; better put it down; the coffee table's right in front of me . . .

Juice all over my lap, my legs, the carpet. Jenny runs to the kitchen for a cloth and starts mopping me up. 'Good thing it was apple juice,' she says cheerfully, 'it shouldn't stain like orange. Your shorts are pretty wet, though—do you want to change?'

'I'm right.' I'd rather sit here damp and pretend it didn't happen. Pretend I didn't see the look on Caroline's face as she sat, frozen and embarrassed, totally unable to handle it. Sick and shaky is okay for hospital, but now I'm home I'm supposed to be me—me with broken bones, but not spastic. Caroline likes rules, and I've broken this one.

'Dad,' says Matt, 'if Ben went to obeying school he'd learn not to jump up, wouldn't he?'

'Obedience classes! Well, yes—that's the theory.'

'So can we go?'

'I'll look into it,' Dad promises weakly.

It's the first time I've talked to Hayden on the phone, and it feels so good—so normal—just like any other girl talking to her boyfriend. I tell him about Hairy Legs, trying to pull something funny out of my not-so-exciting life, but he's more interested in exactly what the insurance will pay for. 'Even physio afterwards?'

He's not just being polite—he's actually worried about the price of physio and relieved about insurance. *Should I feel guilty that I've been so focussed on my problems that I've never even thought about their cost? Did he think he ought to pay? Anything I say is going to make it worse* ... Ask about life at St Pat's.

Much like life at our school, apparently. Someone suspended for smoking in the library. Assignments being handed out thick and fast; lots of lectures on the importance of structuring your time, planning, motivation—and in case no one had noticed—how important this year's marks are for your future. But don't forget to schedule time to play sport and relax.

And just for a minute he's forgotten to feel bad that I'm not even going to school, much less playing sport, and I can play the normal-girl-and-her-boyfriend game again.

Jenny mightn't have much to say about exactly what went on Saturday night but I'm learning a lot more about Costa. He's not only the sexiest, best-looking man alive, he's also incredibly sensitive and intelligent.

'Especially when you think that English is his second language—can you imagine doing VCE in Greek?'

'At the moment I can hardly imagine doing it in English.'

'He speaks Greek at home with his family, and English the rest of the time. Don't you think being bilingual gives people an extra depth in their character . . . am I carrying on?'

'Carrying on like someone in love.'

She looks down; twists her feet around each other like a six-year-old. 'Funny how it's such a scary word when you think you mean it.'

Every Wednesday night our family's hit by a tidying frenzy: dirty clothes to the laundry, newspapers into the magazine rack, Lego in the bucket—if they're not tidied tonight, Mum swears they'll disappear tomorrow. Mrs Hervey, the cleaning ogre, comes on Thursdays.

Mrs Hervey is small and bustly. She gets to our house at nine, after cleaning her own house, cooking her husband's breakfast, packing his lunch, and taking her dog for a walk— using the fresh air before anyone else has a go at it, she says.

'Well, you poor dear!' she exclaims now. 'You don't do things by halves, do you!' She shakes her head, 'tsk, tsking' sadly as she collects spray bottles from under the sink. The tsking gets worse as she checks through the house.

'Looks like I'm in trouble,' Mum whispers, and she's right.

'I thought you were staying home to have some nice time with your daughter—not to clean the house! You've hardly left anything for me!'

'I haven't washed the kitchen floor,' Mum says meekly.

'As if that'll take me three hours! I'll just have to wash your windows.' The glass is rain-spotted and dusty; Mrs Hervey cheers up again.

And this is the tyrant we've been threatened with for two years! I catch Mum's eye. You never know when a bit of blackmail might come in handy.

'If you ever tell the kids . . . I'll put you on Lego duty for the rest of your life!'

Well, it was worth a try. I settle down in the lounge room with my book. Mum's still fussing around.

'I'm just going to dash to the supermarket,' she says finally. 'I've put the answering machine on, so don't rush to the phone if it rings. And I'll tell Mrs Hervey—just ask her if you want anything.'

'Mum, would you go! I'll be fine.'

'I know . . . be careful.'

'I'm reading, Mum. I don't think the book's going to attack me.'

In forty-five minutes she's back.

'I'm still alive!' I shout, before she can ask.

'Sitting up like Jackie,' Mrs Hervey confirms, 'reading her book the whole time you were gone!'

Read all about it! Year 12 student home almost alone. Reads ten pages in forty-five minutes.

Mum makes coffee and puts out a plate of Anzacs and gingersnaps. Even Mrs Hervey stops for one and a chat.

Mum's going to do weekends at the nursery from now on. She says this way it won't cost much more than when she worked the week and had a reliever for Saturday and Sunday, and Luke comes in to see her most nights after he closes, so she knows exactly how everything's going.

There's something about him—the way he acts as if he's got nothing to prove and doesn't expect that you will either—that makes him an easy person to be with. He doesn't ignore all my bandages and braces, he just acts as if I'm normal anyway; I don't mind him seeing me. 'Do you remember that barbecue at our place?' he asks now. 'Years ago—I must have been about fifteen.'

Can't lie; the blush gives me away. 'I was a bit of a brat then.'

'Actually I saw you more as an instrument of fate, out to destroy my illusions. There I was—I'd had two whole judo lessons and was finally going to make an impression on the world—at least on the other kids at the barbecue. Hadn't counted on a skinny twelve-year-old bringing me down to earth with a bump! Ended my judo career with one swift kick.'

'I didn't *mean* to knock you over! I just didn't have very good control over my kicks yet. Did you really quit judo?'

'Afraid so. I haven't got a great record for sticking at things, have I?'

I don't believe it. Apart from that one morning in hospital, I haven't cried about any of this. Now my eyes are filling up with tears because a guy I hardly know quit judo six years ago. All right, because something I did made him quit.

'You can't take all the credit,' he adds quickly. 'It might have had more to do with Dad leaving us the week after the barbecue. Judo just suddenly didn't seem that relevant.'

Not much to say to that either. Swallow a couple of times; make sure my voice is trustworthy. God, this is ridiculous.

'Anyway, a couple of years ago I discovered Tai Chi. What about you—did you go on with karate?'

'I'm having a little break at the moment.'

'The cast gives you an unfair advantage?'

That smile again, then Mum's here with the account books and I go back to my room.

My thumb and I are going to see the occupational therapist.

'Do you want to go anywhere while we're out?' Mum asks. 'In my *wheelchair*?'

But Mum still feels it's a milestone. My first week anniversary of coming home; first time out somewhere. She bakes a cinnamon cake.

'When you said you'd go out with me—did you really mean it? Like, you'd actually go out in a car with me again when you're better?'

He was here all afternoon but he and Dad ended up watching the cricket and in the ads he just talked about karate. At least now we're alone, separated by nothing but the few kilometres of telephone wire between his lounge room and my parents' bedroom.

'I wouldn't have said it if I hadn't meant it.'

'You know what really gets me? If I hadn't slowed down he might have missed us completely!'

Flashes of images; a collage of movie scenes. The concentration on his face, the competence of his hands on the wheel, details imprinted on my brain. Realising we were wrong; knowing I was going to die.

'Or if I'd passed that truck when I had the chance, we'd have been past that corner before he got there.'

'And if I'd never been born I wouldn't have been in the car at all! Look; it happened—like an act of God or something—you're the Catholic, you work it out. But I still want to go out with you ... hang on a second.' I'm suddenly so cold that I have to wrap myself in Mum and Dad's doona before I can go on. My teeth are chattering.

Hayden doesn't sound much better. Actually I think he's crying. He says goodnight and hangs up. If I could escape from my cage for just a minute I'd run all the way to his house and hold him, nothing more, simply hug and be close to him. But if I could escape I guess he wouldn't be crying.

Is there some parallel universe where those things did happen? Where a foolhardy Hayden raced the speeding car, flying through the intersection a second ahead of it? Is the Anna of that universe still living in a normal body in a normal world— and does she know how lucky she is?

Mr Sandberg drops in again Monday.

'How's the life of leisure?'

'Just what I always wanted,' I say, as my slave brings coffee and biscuits and shoos away two outsize flies.

'And how did you go with the work Jenny brought you?'

No snappy answers for that one.

'Anything specific I can help you with?'

I can't concentrate. Nothing goes in. I refuse to say that, but can't think of anything else.

'She's not quite up to it yet,' Mum says defensively. 'But you've been reading for English, haven't you, Anna?'

Hope he doesn't ask which book. I've read quite a bit of it—just can't remember the title.

'Give yourself a break—oh, I see you already have.'

Groan.

'Seriously—you haven't been out of hospital for all that long; we don't need to start worrying about assignments yet. Just relax—tell yourself you're reading for pleasure. Might as well enjoy the lazy life while you can.'

I know it's the only thing I can do. I know he's being helpful. But reading for pleasure is not the same as getting through Year 12.

Haven't heard from Caroline since the day she came over with Jenny.

Why do I feel people have to call me? I'm not such an invalid I can't dial myself. Just do it.

But it's a bad time: she'll call back later.

Later this week, I guess.

Call the *Guinness Book of Records*! Throw a party and put my picture in 'You Can Do it, Girl!' for *Modern Ms*: I've made coffee for Hayden and me. A week ago I tried and wasn't strong enough.

'You couldn't lift a *kettle*?'

'The point is I can do it now! Do you want some cake? Caroline's mum brought a banana one today.'

He likes the cake, but maybe he should have skipped the caffeine, wandering around the room till he makes me dizzy.

'Would you sit down! You're as bad as Matthew!'

He sits obediently and begins picking up and turning over the magazines on the coffee table.

'How was karate yesterday?'

'Okay; mostly sparring again.' I get the feeling that wasn't what he'd intended to say.

'Isn't there a tournament coming up soon?'

'Well, yeah.' The magazines are now all neatly upside down.

'Are you going?'

'Would you mind?'

'I told you before! Why should you give up because some dickhead broke my neck?'

'I thought it might make you feel bad.'

'I'll feel worse if you don't go.'

'You're great, you know that?'

'I know.'

'Could I have a glass of cordial? I don't actually like coffee.'

'So why do you always drink it here? Do you think Mum won't let you come back if you don't like her coffee?'

How can a sheepish grin be sexy? If he kissed me would I stop being obsessed?

My big treat today is a trip to Mr Osman—and as Mum parks right in front of his clinic, I can walk in myself—no wheelchair!

We're going to have to wait a while. His waiting room is packed. I've never seen so many broken people—at least, people with broken bits—in one place before.

'How's the pain?' Mr Osman asks.

So strong, so overwhelming and constant that I can't remember life before it. My body is a vocabulary of hurting; I need shades of meaning to describe the screaming shriek of my neck, the exquisite torture up the back of my skull, the dull grind of the thumb and the fierce jab of a ten-centimetre nail spearing my heel.

'Not bad,' I say.

March already—first term more than half gone!—and evenings are getting darker again; Matt and Bronny are watching a sitcom before they go to bed. Gross adults and cute kids are stuck in another unbelievable predicament, blaring canned laughter and sentimentality. Mum and Dad say they hate it—but follow enough from behind their paper and book to snort in disgust. I don't bother pretending. The slippery surface of my mind is content with the meaningless action, the empty words which don't expect to leave a trace.

An ad break; Mum puts the kettle on.

'Look, Anna!' Matt shouts. 'A girl with a collar like yours!'

Cut from the sound of smashing glass to a girl with a scarred face crying as she struggles to stand up from her wheelchair. It's an ad from the traffic insurance, meant to terrify—I wonder if Trevor Jones is watching. I wonder if I'm going to throw up. Dad grabs for the remote control and knocks it under the couch. The ad goes on as he scrambles.

Bronwyn's voice is cloudy with tears. 'How did they get there so fast?' she asks. 'To make the film?'

'Will they make one of you, Anna?' Matt wants to know.

'That girl's an actor,' Mum explains. 'It's just pretend. Look at her arms—if it were real they'd be cut like Anna's. The scratches on her face are just makeup.' *It's obviously not the first time Mum's watched this ad in fascinated horror.*

Bronwyn's face is still pale and pinched. 'Come and sit on my lap,' I beg.

Delicately, she leans over and gives me a hug, the butterfly embrace of one frail old woman to another. 'I'll hurt you,' she says, and has a cuddle from Mum instead.

Just as well—I've got the shakes again. My coffee slops darkly over my shirt.

'Caroline! It's so great to see you!' *And such a surprise that I feel ridiculously flustered.* 'Do you want a coffee?'

'I've given up caffeine—it's amazing how much better you feel when you get all those toxins out of your system.'

Guess I won't put out the Mississippi Mud Cake. 'So how's everything at school?'

'I hate my new home room—you know I'm not with you guys this year? And school's such a drag without you there, you better come back soon or I'll go crazy! There's no one to talk to!'

'Aren't you talking to Jenny any more?'

'You have to be named Costa if you want to talk to Jenny right now.'

'Meow, meow.'

'No really, it's sweet. But we all miss you; our last year together—we just want you back!'

So I go into my happy little vegemite act. I feel great, it hardly hurts at all; this frame is just a nuisance really—a precaution—doctors have to be so careful, don't they? And the cast, well nothing could hurt inside that! I'll be back at school in about four weeks.

A question mark flits at the back of my mind. It's four weeks since the accident—will I really be better, school-better, in another four?

But there was all that time wasted when they didn't know my neck was broken. Now that everything's sorted out it'll happen fast. School the beginning of April, Black Belt in October. If you want something badly enough, you always get there in the end.

CHAPTER 6

My thumb is the first to let me down.

It's done so many exercises it should look like Elle MacPherson—but after three weeks of workouts it still can't tell the difference between 'bend as tight as you can' and standing up straight.

'Twenty-five degrees,' Mr Osman says, and studies the new X-rays.

Twenty-five degrees is what the therapist said the first time she measured it.

'The bone's healed well,' Mr Osman says now, 'unfortunately . . .'

Unfortunately the joint in the middle of the thumb—the one that wasn't supposed to be damaged—is affected too. Stuffed, though that's not the word he uses.

'You'll have arthritis in it, of course. If the pain gets too bad we'll operate and freeze it into a better position. In the meantime the OT can make you a splint.'

He hesitates. *Arthritis, operations—hasn't he run out of bad news yet?* 'It's an unusual break; I've never seen one just like it. Were you holding anything in your hand?

A trophy.

If he says something funny I'll kick him with my fat plaster foot. But he thinks about it and nods. He's satisfied.

I'm seventeen. I refuse to think about arthritis. I'll worry about that if I manage to get old.

The splint looks obscene. I think it's only my dirty mind, but Jenny gets the giggles when she sees it. Even Dad hides a smile.

'Only use this to do the exercises,' Julie said when she gave it to me. 'Don't wear it all the time.'

I think I'll be able to restrain myself.

Caroline hasn't been to see me again. I ring her occasionally, but it's always a bad time. She's about to go out, or have dinner, or has a friend over.

Hayden's another reason I've got to be better soon. I want to know what he feels about me and what I feel about him. And I don't know how I'm going to find out if we're never alone.

But tonight the kids are in bed, Mum and Dad watching TV in the lounge. Hayden's sitting on the family room floor by my chair; I remember the feel of his hair when he cried in the hospital, and I stroke it again now. Does he remember his head on my breast?

He lifts his arm across my knee and rests his head against it. 'I'm not hurting you?'

'My knees are okay.'

Why do I think about sex now, when my body's trapped and undesirable?

Very lightly, he strokes the inside of my knee, and I have a sudden flash of memory—the last thing I want to think about right now—of Hayden putting his hand on my leg as we drove, and my laughing and returning it to the wheel, then crossing my legs away from him, for emphasis. The right knee crossed over the left, the right foot against the door. Seconds before we saw the white car.

So that's why my right foot was smashed worse than the left. I'd wondered about that.

Two hands on the wheel didn't help anyway. I should have left his hand where it was.

How could Luke quit uni after doing two whole years? How can he bear not knowing where his life's going now? Just drifting, letting things happen; working in Mum's nursery could hardly be a long-term ambition.

'Sometimes it's not such a bad way to go,' he says, 'seeing where life takes you.'

'But how can you plan anything?' *Because that's one of the worst things about the way I'm living now—not knowing for sure exactly how soon I'll be back to normal and able to organise my life again.*

'Sometimes it's good to go without plans.'

'So you don't have to change them when things go wrong?'

'That's a bit negative! More like the difference in philosophy behind karate and Tai Chi.'

'You've lost me.'

'Karate's goal-directed—if it's an opponent, you hit them; if it's a brick or a plank or whatever, you break it, right?'

'That's the general idea!'

'Tai Chi is more inner-directed; it can be used as a martial art but it's based on Taoism . . . if you think of life as a river, no matter how huge a boulder is, the river flows around it—might have to change course a bit, but it still gets where it's going—and the rock gradually gets worn away.'

'Doesn't sound like much of an adrenalin rush!' *Which is the best part of karate, even something as artificial as brick-chopping—part of your mind knows that it's impossible to smash that brick with your bare hand, and the rest of you knows that you can, and you concentrate, visualise—and let loose and do it, do the impossible . . .*

He's grinning. 'So what are you breaking now?'

'My plaster,' I admit—*does he read everyone's mind, or just mine?* 'You still haven't told me why you left uni.'

He shrugs. 'Business studies was bad enough, but when I got into the advertising stream I really started to hate it. Every assignment was worse; in the end I could barely force myself to do them—it was all completely alien to the way I think.

Why should I want to manipulate people's minds to buy what I want?'

'So why'd you do it in the first place?'

'I thought it would be something my dad and I could share—he's totally wrapped up in his work. Pretty mature, eh? I was going to live with him, get to know him ... maybe I even wanted to be like him, strange as it sounds.'

'Not that strange—he's pretty successful.'

'He's paid a price for it! Which is okay for him, it's his choice—but it's not mine. I figure there has to be something more important than money and power, prestige and all that; eventually I realised that it was my life and I'd have to work out what to do with it myself. It didn't exactly improve my relationship with my dad, but I guess that's the price *I* have to pay.'

I'm not sure about his 'life as a river' theory, but at least he's open and honest—no bull! When he's talking about something serious his eyes go dark—then suddenly he's teasing again and they go back to that deep, brilliant blue.

FLD. Foot Liberation Day.

I follow Mr Osman out to a back room, with shelves of instruments. The power saw is the one that grabs my eye. It must be the reason the floor's linoleum—bloodstains are a nightmare on carpet.

The ferocious saw whirrs and whines, slicing the plaster but—miraculously—not me. My right leg looks like a plant that's been growing under a rock, skinny, white and wrinkled. It feels light and free.

I've brought my right sneaker in a bag; I put it on and parade up and down the hall—*I'm walking, I'm normal!*—while Mr Osman watches, frowning.

'I'll write you a referral for physio,' he says.

Jeans! With the fat foot gone I can wear what I like—the bottom half, anyway. Maybe I'm even glad that they're the old pair, the ones that weren't cut off in Casualty. I feel more like me in well-worn denim.

When my foot touches the floor in the morning it feels as if some idiot's come along and hammered spikes up through the floor boards. Looks like it'll take a while to get used to not having the plaster. I still walk like a baby, legs straddled wide across an invisible nappy, arms out for balance.

'Come in three times a week,' physio Brian says, grunting with the effort of trying to yank my ankle into the shape he wants. When he's exhausted he lends me a wooden rocking board so I can practise at home. Just a few minutes, he says, three times a day.

Bend, stretch, pull it up, point it down, swivel in circles. Looks so easy when Brian's foot does it.

Coming home from physio I'm tired. That's my excuse anyway. I miss the doorway to the kitchen; hit my shoulder, scrape my thumb. *Sticking out like a sore thumb.* Such a stupid expression; such a stupid-looking thumb. Weak, red and stiff; wouldn't be so bad except when you think of it being like that forever. Or worse.

But compared to the other things . . .

I offer my thumb up as a sacrifice, a bargain with God or whoever makes the rules: I won't complain about my thumb, if you heal my ankles and my neck.

Jenny on the phone, 'What's that tapping?'

It's the ankle-rocking board. My parents are always complaining about how long Jenny and I talk—at least now I'm doing something useful at the same time.

'I knew you'd be happy once you got some exercises!'

But you don't know what happy is till you can't do something normal and you learn to do it again. This morning Sally was curled up on my armchair—so I sat on the couch. Even better, a while later I managed to get off it!

And now the ultimate test. The seat where you really like to be normal; move the frame and try . . .

I can use the toilet!

Luke's got a tray of unhappy baby betonies for Mum to inspect and—with a bit of luck—nurse back to health in her 'hospital' behind the carport. Its benches are overflowing with cuttings and seedlings again, now that she trusts me not to fall off my chair and die the instant she gets her fingers into a tub of compost. Luke comes in to say hi when he's deposited the patients, and we're talking—actually I'm listening, and he's offering me morsels of his day: the guy who jumped to conclusions at the sight of Luke's long hair and wanted to know when to transplant marijuana seedlings; the lady who brought her cat in to help choose the right catnip—when Bronwyn comes in with Hayden.

A pang of guilt at not hearing him knock. It seems strange they haven't met before; I want them to like each other. Bronny leans against my shoulder, twining a foot around the leg of my chair, and we watch as they talk; they're both standing and their presence seems to fill the room—Hayden taller and restless, shifting his weight from foot to foot as he says something about doing surveying next year; Luke responding with his direct gaze and quiet intensity, the expression on his face harder to read.

'He's okay,' Hayden decides when Luke's gone, 'but—no offence to your mum—isn't that a bit of a dead-end job?'

'Not if it gives him time to work out what he really wants to do; he figures if he keeps an open mind the right thing will just turn up.'

'I don't know. He'd have been better off to finish his course and get a proper job even if he wasn't crazy about it; seems

stupid to waste two years at uni and have nothing to show
for it.'

It's ten in the morning. I've been reading for half an hour—a.
in understanding and remembering, not my usual brain-dead
staring.

A break, a coffee with Mum, thumb exercises; ankle exercises; pick up the book again. Ten minutes this time, then my
brain goes walkabout.

The afternoon's normal—as in back to brain-dead.

But it worked this morning. I've got to try. I've missed six
weeks of school already—forty minutes a day is not enough
Mr Sandberg's last visit: 'You might have to think about doing
Year 12 over two years.' Push that out of my head and go on
reading. Try having the radio on ... follow the music instead
of the writing. Try earplugs ... instant mini amplifiers for the
ringing in my ears.

Ignore it; concentrate; what's happened to your willpower?
You've got to go on reading.

I can't see. My neck's doing its gnawed-by-a-crocodile
imitation, and everything's gone black. *If I sit very still I won't*
fall off the chair ... I just wanted to sit here and read! Is that
so much to ask? I'm not giving in!

I have to. It's that or black out.

I call Mum to help me take off my frame and go to bed.

But I tried—I really tried. I used every ounce of willpower.
What am I supposed to do now?

Jenny and Costa are going out together. It's official—not that
there seems to have been any doubt in Jenny's mind since the
first time she spoke to him. What's amazing is that it became
official after she took him clothes shopping. The door of a
dress shop acts as a sort of catalytic converter on Jen—instant
whirlwind. Any guy who could stand outside the changing
room for long enough for her to try on the entire size twelve

stock in the shop would have to be either in a coma or in love.

'Oh, he didn't mind.'

'He read *War and Peace* while he waited?'

'Very funny. He actually chose this shirt. Anyway, you *have* to meet him now—it feels too weird having a boyfriend that you haven't even met!'

'What am I, the boyfriend monitor?'

'My dad's already applied for that. No, come on, why don't you call Hayden and we'll all go for coffee.'

'How about we wait till I'm not wearing a set of monkey bars around my neck?'

'How about you stop being such a wimp? You still look like Anna, you know—a normal person with a metal brace. It doesn't turn you into a freak.'

'You're a bully, Jen! Okay. Hayden's got a tournament this weekend . . . next Saturday. I promise.'

Sunday morning I wake up ready to try something. Mum hardly has to lift at all any more to get me out of bed, so . . . roll to the side, push with my right arm . . . I'm sitting up! Dance, sing, throw a party. Better yet, call Bronwyn; tell her how to help me with the frame.

'You *are* getting better!' she shouts.

Did she ever doubt it? Did she think I'd be locked in a metal brace, lifted up and down, all my life?

It's just a broken bone, I tell her. A broken bone in your neck is scarier than a broken leg, but it heals exactly the same way. In a couple of months I'll be good as new.

Bronwyn's not listening. She's screaming through the house to wake Mum and Dad, 'Anna sat up by herself!'

'How was the tournament?'

'Okay.'

I guess he didn't win. 'Do you want to come over?'

'I've got a heap of homework . . .'

'. . . Mum's made a chocolate orange cake . . .'

'I don't feel like doing it anyway. See you in a minute.'

'To see me or the chocolate cake?'

'Don't make me choose!'

But he's had his cake now and I still haven't heard about the tournament. (And here I am, under house arrest and getting desperate for news of the outside world!)

'Who did you fight first?'

'David Someone, tall guy from Melbourne.'

'I remember him. You should have beaten him, didn't you?'

'Yeah. Got warned on contact.'

'Must have been a strict judge—you never get warnings! I hardly ever seem to make it through a tournament without one.'

'Well, I made up for it this time.'

'What did you do, kill someone?'

'I could have. The guy I fought in the next round was named Trevor. I had this flash about how I'd feel if it was Trevor Jones—I knocked him down on the first point and I went on hitting him . . . I'm quitting karate.'

'But you're good, Hayden—you're bound to get on the state team this year—you can't quit just because you stuffed up once!'

'Listen, I'm telling you I totally lost it. You be a macho karate dickhead if you want—I've had enough!'

The back door slams; he's gone.

'What's a macho karate dickhead?' asks Matt.

'Never mind.'

'Is Hayden still your boyfriend?'

'Mind your own business, Bronwyn.'

'How could he say that?' I ask Jenny.

She's trying hard not to laugh—not completely successfully. 'Maybe because you treat karate like the world's answer to religion, education and social life, all rolled up into one. But I'm sure he didn't mean it—just forget it. Kiss and make up.'

'I wish he would!'

But Hayden's not the first guy to quit a martial art because of me, so when Luke comes to see Mum the next day I ask him what he thinks.

'He's not quitting because of you—it's his own anger he's afraid of.'

'But he's angry because I got hurt.'

'It's still *his* anger. He's got to face it some time.'

Mum's coming in from the washing line, but there's one more thing I've got to ask—'Do you think I'm a macho karate dickhead?'

'You really expect me to answer that?' Then the teasing evaporates; his eyes darken into their serious expression and he puts his hand on my arm as he adds, 'The guy cares about you, Anna—and he's hurting. You'll have to sort it out, one way or another.'

He comes back to see me before he leaves. 'Have you done it yet?'

'Right! I just jogged there and back!'

'And the telephone's out of order?'

'Go away.'

The problem is, Luke's right. Hayden was really hurting, and I didn't try very hard to understand. I shut myself in Mum and Dad's bedroom and dial. He was just going to call me; he's sorry he said what he did.

'Are you really quitting?'

'Don't start!'

'I just wondered.'

'I don't know.'

I think we're still together.

CHAPTER 7

The beginning of independence. I wake up as excited as Matt at Christmas—today's the day I get out of bed all by myself, nothing on my neck but the foam bedtime collar. Walk to the mirror. My head doesn't fall off.

'Decrease the frame gradually,' Mr Osman said yesterday. 'In a month you should be wearing the collar all the time.'

I'm in the shower. All alone; nobody helping, nobody watching; I can even sing if I want! My plastic bag leaks, the collar's soggy and my neck's ready for a rest by the time I'm dry, but I don't care. The district nurse has just been fired.

Even my toast tastes better when my jaw's not propped up by metal struts.

'But I'm used to you with it on,' Matthew objects. 'This one looks stupid.'

Dad's sister Lynda's come up from Melbourne this week. 'I love March up here; you feel like you want to get out there and grab the last bit of summer! Do you people realise how lucky you are, having the river right at your back gate?'

'That's why we bought it,' Dad says dryly.

What wouldn't I give to go with her, to scramble through the undergrowth to the path, climb over the enormous bleached log whose top branches stretch far enough over the river that you can climb out and jump straight in to swim . . .

But I can only just make it across the back yard without falling.

Which Lynda hasn't taken long to spot. That's the problem with having a nurse in the house for a few days—lots of time for her to sit and observe.

'You're dizzy, aren't you?'

'Not that bad. You get used to it.'

'You keep pretending you've just got out of Luna Park? God, Anna, you must be mad as hell about all this! How do you cope with it?'

'I try not to think about it.'

'Great idea—repress it all and give yourself cancer! Sorry, kid, but you'll have to look at it eventually. I'll leave you a few books that might help.'

I've phoned Caroline and she's coming over. So simple—I don't know why I wasted time being tense.

Because now that she's here, she's smiling, laughing, chattering. I'm looking a lot better now, must be great to have that plaster off; have I heard that the Year 10 boys all shaved their heads to go on camp? Look like dags, can you believe it? And she's trying out for the production of *Oliver*; thinks she's got a good chance of getting the part of Nancy. It's a fair commitment, but she's sure she can handle it without letting her grades drop.

'Though they don't slack off the work requirements or give you any special help if you've got in-school commitments, not like when you're having a sickie.'

It slides in and out like a knife; slipped in so sweetly, in the same breath with the gossip, that it takes me a moment to feel the sting. The savagery.

I'm numb. I don't think I can speak—but as she leaves I hear my automatic, 'See you later.'

Caroline pulls out her school diary and flips through it; the mask has slipped, she's frantic, panicky—'I don't know what I'm doing next week.'

So am I supposed to make an appointment?

But now I know for sure—the viciousness wasn't a slip of the tongue. She hates me.

She was my friend. A friend who shared secrets; who brought me flowers; who wiped the blood from my legs.

I always knew that if I ever started to cry I'd never be able to stop, and now I've started and it's true, there's so much sadness, so much misery inside me and it won't stop till there's nothing left of me. These tears aren't coming from my eyes, they're pouring out of my soul, out of every bit of my body, my blood and my muscles and right down to my bone marrow where the deepest, harshest grief has been buried. I didn't think I could feel like this and still live, but the misery, the tears, and the terrible wailing noise keep on going, and I think maybe this is what hell is, to know that your life is out of control and there's nothing you can do about it.

Ben's howling outside in echo; Matt and Bronny are peering round my door, Bronny clutching Sally so tightly that the cat's yowling too—I know I'm scaring them, but the misery is stronger than I am.

'I just didn't want this to happen! I *didn't* want it to happen.'

'No one did,' Mum says, shooing the kids away. 'Anna needs to cry,' she tells them. 'It'll be good for her.'

She's wrong. Feeling this terrible can't be good for anyone— I *hate* crying, and I'm not going to do it again.

You can't open a paper or turn on the TV without hearing about euthanasia. The whole world's obsessed with it. And everyone's so adamant, whichever side they're on! They're all so sure they'd rather be dead than disabled—or just as convinced that God meant the person to suffer through and learn something. (Learn what? If God's so smart can't he work out a better way to teach? And how much pain is too much; how do you decide?)

One thing I know—if I was going to have this much pain, this many restrictions every day of my life, I'd be on the first bus to the Northern Territory.

I'm afraid to tell Jenny about Caroline. I don't know what I'm guilty of, but I feel so ashamed—and scared. Maybe Jenny will drop me too.

Good to be wrong occasionally.

Her eyes are watering; her face is pink and set with rage. 'How can she be like that?' she keeps repeating. 'God, I feel bad enough that my life is so great when yours is so shitty! How can she make it *worse*?'

'Maybe she thinks I'm getting too much attention . . . I should tell her I could do without it!'

She hesitates, wheels turning—you can always tell when Jenny's trying to decide whether or not to say something. 'She's talked once or twice about how much money people make when they have an accident—from suing the other driver.'

My throat's so dry I can hardly speak. 'But that's only if you're permanently disabled and'—the tears squeak through my voice—'there's no money on earth that could make that worthwhile.'

'That's what I told her! Look—if she's acting like this she wasn't ever a real friend anyway; at least now we know what she's like.'

But Jenny's wrong. You can't throw away five years like that. Thinking that she was never my friend is even worse.

I hope Jenny will forget about going out on Saturday, but no such luck. She says she'll ring Hayden herself if I don't ask him—but I called him last time.

It's Friday night when he finally phones. 'What've you been up to?'

Physio, doctor, being dumped by a friend . . . 'Not much. Listen—instead of sticking around the house all weekend, do you want to meet Jenny and Costa at the Coffee Connection tomorrow?'

Bronny and Vinita are flitting around in their leotards again when he picks me up—Dad asked Bronny to change ages ago, but here they are again, giggling, now that Hayden's here . . . 'They've got a crush on you!'

Hayden blushes and starts the car. 'Don't be stupid!'

Eight million eyes in one small cafe. Why does Jenny think this is good for me? Couldn't I do something simple like bungie jumping?

At least Costa's nice—or Jenny's briefed him well, or both. He manages to look me in the face when we meet, and finds us a table near the back so I don't put everyone off as they walk in the door. He and Hayden go up to the counter to order and Jenny leans across the table to whisper.

'So what do you think?'

'Definitely a guy, and you're right, his eyes are brown. I'll need a few more minutes for the full psychic profile.'

'Is everything okay with you and Hayden now?'

'I guess so. Well, we're here—it must be.'

'You know we could hear every word you said?' Costa says, sliding into the seat beside Jenny.

'Liar.'

She smacks his leg, he grabs her hand, and they sit there frozen for a moment, staring into each other's eyes, and it's as intimate and embarrassing as if we'd walked in on them naked. Maybe not quite. Don't think about it.

'Who wants a chip?' I suggest, and Jenny and Costa wake up. But their hands stay joined so Jenny has to drink her milkshake with her left hand.

'Where'd you live before?' Hayden asks.

'Sydney—Coogee. Could have done without changing school systems this year, but'—he looks at Jenny—'sometimes you've got to be unlucky to be lucky.'

'You left Sydney for *Yarralong*?'

'My dad got a chance at a franchise here—he'd only ever be a manager in Sydney. My mum thought a country town would be safer for my sisters—and there's a big enough Greek community to have a church, so she's happy.'

I have a feeling Coogee's on the sea. 'So do you surf?'

'Not any more! I keep taking my board down to the river, waiting for the swell . . . never seems to come up.'

'It's good for swimming,' Jenny says loyally.

'You and your river,' Costa teases, and they're off on another of those looks. His arm's around her shoulders now, his fingers stroking her neck under her hair, straying across her shoulders, while she relaxes and leans into him—their bodies look so *comfortable* together! On our side of the table, Hayden and I are sitting up good-children-straight; I'm on the right and I know he's too scared of hurting my thumb to hold my left hand, but I wish I had the nerve to rest my hand on his thigh, to do anything to be a couple like they are. Instead Hayden goes up for another coke, and I finish my coffee; it's hard to think of anything to say when the others have forgotten we're here.

Sometimes I feel so cheated. I'm not taking time off—I've had a whole chunk of my life stolen. Nobody's going to hand me a few months at the other end and say, 'Here you are, here's the bit you missed out on.'

The wheelchair's leaving. Cleaned; folded; packed into the boot of Dad's car like a guilty secret. *Tough luck, chair—I win, you lose—I'm not a cripple after all.*

'Keep it a bit longer, Anna,' Matt wheedles. 'You might need it!' He and Bronwyn have invented wheelchair surfing in the carport—one person stands on the seat; the other gives it a running push. Whoever falls off least wins.

'Or *you* might,' says Dad. 'Maybe we could go for a hat trick—all three of you with broken necks!'

Mum bakes an apple cake to see it off.

But physio Brian isn't celebrating. He's not happy about the way I'm walking. I don't like it much either—like carrying my own personal bed of nails; one goes through my foot each time I step on it.

He's more worried about the deformed way I it put down. And how I put all the weight on my left leg. He's worried about the damage I'm doing to my hips and knees.

'Shit, Brian, my hips are the only things I didn't hurt!'

'So let's keep it that way.' And he hands me a stick. A walking stick, a cane. Like old people use.

'Or anyone that breaks a leg!' he says. 'Come on, the important thing here is to get you walking properly again.'

'But I didn't have one at first! I feel like I'm going backwards.'

'You weren't fit enough to hold anything at first,' he snaps. 'And you weren't moving around much, either. Now let me get the right height for you, and you can have a little practice.'

My stick is dark brown wood, the handle dips so that I can hold it without hurting my thumb. It's polished smooth and absolutely plain.

When I walk out into the street after physio I feel as if it glows like a neon sign, a three-metre barber's pole flashing white and red with a siren on top. People stop what they're doing to stare open-mouthed at the freak teenager with a stick.

'It's not that bad,' Jenny tries to convince me. 'It's nothing like the neck brace.'

'But that's temporary; I'll be getting rid of it soon. A stick makes me look disabled—spastic!'

The very worst thing about the stick—and I don't even admit this to Jen—is that it helps. My foot doesn't hurt so much, I walk better—and I'm not as dizzy, though that's so strange I don't even like admitting it to myself.

Just when I think life couldn't get worse, Mum brings up what Mr Sandberg said about doing Year 12 over two years. Sensible, she says. The pits, I say: everyone going off to uni or whatever—and me still stuck in school with the Year 11s.

Maybe I could catch up if I had tutoring.

Mr Sandberg comes up with two names and Mum arranges appointments. Lisa Harris arrives that afternoon, complete with baby in a pram.

'I couldn't get a sitter at such short notice,' she says.

Mum doesn't seem to mind. Babies always make her go slightly soft in the head; she goos and peek-a-boos while Lisa and I struggle with maths and psychology.

'Twice a week?' Lisa suggests. 'We've got a bit of catching up to do.'

Which is a polite way of saying that she's noticed I haven't actually started the year's work yet.

'And little Miss Becky,' she adds, taking the baby back from Mum, holding her over her face and planting a kiss on the fat tummy, 'will go to her babysitter or we'll never get anything done!' Her voice has changed to a special mother to baby voice—for an instant they're as isolated and complete as Jenny and Costa at the Coffee Connection.

I çan see Mum dying to offer—but she remembers in time that she's going back to work and won't always be here to play with babies.

The English and Lit tutor is Martin Weiss. He's short and wiry, about twenty-eight, and a sailor—a sail-boat sailor, not navy. He's just returned from taking a friend's boat from Florida to Seattle; I'd rather hear about the trip—through the Panama

Canal, detour to the Galapagos Islands and Hawaii—than English.

He'll come twice a week too. Then there's physio three times a week, doctor or OT every couple of weeks—and somehow I've got to fit in school after the Easter break.

For Dad's birthday Mum makes French onion soup. Bronwyn's helping. She's wearing her most serious expression, a huge red apron—and her swimming goggles.

'Peeling onions makes me cry,' she says.

'Have you ever thought about meditating?' Luke asks, as we're waiting for Mum to come back from the supermarket and sort out a confusion over whether she had meant to add the extra zero when she ordered a hundred and twenty concrete sundials.

'You don't think I've got enough to do?'

'I just figured you were fighting pain the whole time—if you could give yourself a break, you might have a little more energy left over.'

'You're saying I can *think* the pain away?'

'What have you got to lose? Next time you have a rest, try visualising the pain—like a red mist, or a black liquid, whatever you like, and let it soak out of your body.'

I could almost imagine it while he's talking. He's got a voice like a singer, deep but gentle—or maybe it's just the sincerity that makes it so attractive. Or the surprise—you never know what he's going to come up with next.

'How do you think of this stuff?'

'I had a friend with a brain tumour. He told me.'

'*Had?* Did he . . . '

'No. He moved to Perth.'

Dad comes home unexpectedly at lunchtime, pale and rather red around the eyes. He kisses me as well as Mum. Not normal.

'Jim Meissing came in this morning,' he says. 'Did you know his son died a fortnight ago?'

Mum goes white; starts stroking my shoulder as if she doesn't know she's doing it. 'How?'

'Car accident.'

'And Jim still came in for his appointment?'

Dad shrugs. 'Going through the motions. I don't think he understood one thing I said about his accounts; we just talked about his son.'

'An accident like mine?' *Victim or murderer?*

But it was a single-vehicle accident—high speed into a tree. No trace of drugs or alcohol in his system, his father said—simply a mistake in judgement.

I don't want to do this. My stomach's tensing and my head pounding. I'm not ready.

Mum pulls up in front of the Senior Wing. Chris and Thula spot us and charge towards the car. Too late; can't chicken out now.

'Jenny said you'd be here today!'

'Back in time for the holidays!'

'Only for home room.'

'Great idea. I think I'll try that too.'

'God, you're so skinny!'

'Come on, we'll go over now. Can you walk that far?'

'How long do you have to wear that collar for? Is it better than that metal thing? That must have been the pits!'

Conversation swirls, too hard to catch; I'm concentrating on walking. Don't want to fall over, my first day at school. I'd never noticed how uneven this path is. Funny the things your body takes for granted, when everything's working the way it's meant to.

Twenty-five people makes fifty eyes and they're all on me. I know them all, this shouldn't be so hard—*thank God Caroline's in the other class this year*—but everyone thinks I should be better now, they want me to be better, they're my friends—but I'm not better, I'm a fraud and a failure. Hurry up, Mr Sandberg, this was your bright idea.

Here he is, welcomes me with the 'little break' joke I expected. On through the daily rubbish. A reminder that the school colours are green and gold and that any hair accessories must conform or be confiscated. (*I came back for this?*)

'Sorry, Jason—I know how much your pink hair ribbons mean to you.'

Which is meant to show us that he thinks the rule is as dumb as we do. Thula's getting worked up about the pettiness of dress rules. Jenny and Costa are trapped somewhere in each other's eyes—I don't think they're worrying about hair accessories. Brad is folding a paper aeroplane. Mia thinks we should get up a petition. I'm a hundred years old, listening from another planet.

The bell goes; I stay where I am as everyone rushes past, goodbye, great to see you, see you soon, have a great Easter.

After all that the real work—the meeting with Mr Sandberg and my tutors—is easy. Actually a bit pointless. They'll have to contact the subject teachers later; and we already know that I need to catch up a term's work. I think Mr Sandberg just decided it would be good for me to come into the school for a morning.

Great. Done that. Now can I please get better?

Hayden hasn't been to karate all week. He says he hasn't made up his mind yet. Funny how hard it is not to say anything, sometimes.

Bronwyn comes in with her arm in a sling.

'What happened?' Hayden asks. He hasn't seen her in a sling as often as I have.

'My finger's sore. I think it's infected.'

'It's a mosquito bite,' I say, but Hayden studies it seriously.

'Kiss it better!' Matt teases, hopping out of the way as Bronny rushes at him in fury.

Hayden winks at me. 'Do you want me to put out the rubbish?' he asks, and lunges at Matt, who squeals and leaps over the back of the couch; Hayden follows with Bronwyn swinging off one hand. The couch topples over.

Hayden shoves it upright as Dad rushes in. 'What's going on? Are you kids bothering Anna and Hayden?'

They're still giggling as Hayden and I escape for a walk. 'Don't take your stick,' he says. 'You can lean on me.' We reach the footpath and he takes my hand. It sends warm shock waves through me, the feel of his fingers around mine. They're strong, square hands; his skin's a bit rough. They feel just the way a man's hands should feel.

'You're good with the kids,' I say. 'They really like you.'

'I'm used to kids; I reckon it's an advantage of having a big family. It'd be good, one day . . . ' His voice trails off. I realise I'm holding my breath. 'You want to have kids, don't you?' he asks.

'Not right now!'

'No, but you know—one day?'

Does he mean with him? He'll have to kiss me then . . .

'One day. When I've worked for a while and got my black belt, travelled through Europe—I want to cycle around Holland and meet my mum's relatives . . . all that stuff.' *The pictures go on at the back of my mind: living with Hayden, travelling with him, being together. We've already been through so much; nothing else could be quite so hard.*

We reach the end of the block, shoulders rubbing as we walk. This is the best day we've ever had together. I wish we could go on walking, but we've got a lifetime, when I'm stronger we can be together as much as we want. There's a bench just around the corner. We can sit down for a bit before we go back. 'You know Lisa, my maths tutor? She's a single mum. That'd be so hard.'

'It's wrong.'

'It can't be wrong to have a baby, not if she wants it. She really loves her; she's a good mother.'

'Wrong for the guy, I mean. The father. The baby's his responsibility too—he can't just walk out on it.'

'But—' There are a thousand answers to that, but I let it drop. I'm too happy, sitting here with him, hands joined, knees touching, to worry about the rights and wrongs of other people's problems.

Mum's in the kitchen baking a millionth batch of biscuits, the radio on in the background. I've read a chapter of *Tess of the d'Urbervilles* and finished the first question on Martin's sheet; I deserve a reward by the time Mum calls to say the meringues are out of the oven and she's putting the kettle on.

k.d. lang finishes; an earnest discussion begins. Suicide; teenage suicide especially. Australia the worst of the OECD countries; not a biggest and best statistic to be proud of—and the true figures worse than the records, the speaker explains, because so many suicides are recorded as accidents. 'Much easier on the families that way,' she says. 'Of course it's impossible to prove, but many young men in single-vehicle accidents may in fact be suicides.'

We think of Dad's client's son. No drugs or alcohol, the father had said, just a mistake in judgement.

How do you dig up the nerve to drive into a tree?

And what if it didn't work? If instead of death you got paralysis? Or just ended up like me, crippled with pain and wondering if it'll ever end.

I suppose you could always try again.

Rerun of the kitchen-Mum-mixing-up-biscuits scene.

An indescribable noise, a boom that fills the world, a sound that blacks out light and vision. The stove has exploded—and woken me up. But I know that the noise had nothing to do with exploding stoves—it was the sound of two cars colliding.

How do I know that when I can't remember the accident? Are all those memories tucked in my brain waiting for me to stumble over them?

Jenny's mum's friend the faith healer comes to pray for me again. Mum, agnostic and uncomfortable, welcomes her and whisks promptly out to the garden.

Maybe I'll go too. It's not the praying that's so bad—it's the failing. I was so sure I'd get better fast, last time I met her; now my thumb's stuffed and my ankle's not looking crash-hot either. It gets harder to hope when nothing works out.

But I don't have to believe in something to want it to work. I try and relax into it and nearly do—as the hypnotic voice takes effect I feel the pain starting to float out of my bones. *Is this what Luke was talking about with meditation?*

She finishes and sits quietly, holding my left hand between both of hers. 'You have to stop fighting, Anna, if you're going to let the healing in.'

The warm feeling disappears like a popped balloon. *This is the last faith healing I'm having—the woman's nuts. I'll never stop fighting my injuries; what am I supposed to do— give in?*

CHAPTER 8

'I've been talking to Mark's dad,' Hayden announces without saying hello—Mr Ryan is a policeman who knows more than anyone would ever want to about crashed cars and the smashed people inside them. 'Asked him if we'd have to go to court when Trevor Jones is sentenced.'

So that's why the flush of anger, the set shoulders and thrust jaw. His tension springs to me and snatches, though I'm not sure if mine is rage or fear.

'And do we?' *Exhibit A, the victim . . . I couldn't take it.*

'He doesn't bloody go himself! He does this to you and you know what he gets? An on-the-spot fine! A hundred and sixty-five bucks for failing to give way!'

Is that what my life's worth? A slap on the wrist? Naughty boy, don't kill anyone again. Never mind, it was only Anna.

'. . . bloody dickhead bastard,' Hayden is saying.

Mum, coming in, raises her eyes at the language, but at the explanation, starts swearing under her breath in Dutch.

But Dad's obviously gone into this one too. When we tell him he says, his voice bitter, 'The law looks at it that a $165 fine is a reasonable price for a careless mistake. It's the victim's bad luck if she pays a higher price—the law is interested in his intent, not Anna's luck.'

'Even if I'd died?'

'Apparently. I gather that in that case there would have been a coroner's inquest—but unless he could be charged with culpable driving it'd still be the same—failing to give way and a $165 fine.'

Coroner's not a word you usually associate with yourself. It makes me shudder; Mum too—'It doesn't bear thinking about.'

'That's why I don't care what happens to him,' says Dad, hugging me carefully, 'as long as you're okay.'

Maybe the worst thing is that it's all over for him. Trevor Jones has handed over his $165, and it's all done. (Does he ever get a funny feeling when he drives down that road—'*I wrecked somebody's life here once*'?) It's just for me that it keeps on going. I'm the one trapped in jail.

At least I don't have to go to court—but at the moment it doesn't make me any happier.

Carefully down the three steps and out to the carport. Not really a carport, the car doesn't live here; just bikes, a pingpong table, collection of balls—and my punching bag. The floor-to-ceiling bag I got last Christmas.

I ache to use it. I stroke the smooth leather, letting it shiver gently on its blue elastic cords, poor confused punching bag, waiting for the punch.

So what do I do with my rage, now that I can't hit anything? Now that I can't *do* anything?

I must be in a mood to torture myself. After visiting my punching bag I put on the video of our Christmas karate demonstration.

It's like watching another person. The me on the screen jumps, kicks, spins and punches, her body balanced and precise. Her body knows what it's doing.

And it hits me, like one of the screen-me punches, *that's* what different. It's not that I limp, or that my neck's stiff. It's that my body doesn't know how to move any more. Nothing's natural. Walking's not bad—if it's in a straight line and everything's perfect. Add a challenge like stepping down from a kerb or getting through a doorway—and I need to talk it through like learning a complicated new kata: 'Okay, turn now, brace yourself . . . a bit more to the left.' Thud! 'Damn!' I can't even roll over in bed without waking up to tell myself how.

Then there's losing contact with my knees, if I stand up for some unreasonable time—like more than thirty seconds. Usually I can tell when they're starting to go and sit down fast. If it happens when I'm walking I can sometimes find them by stamping.

Crazy. Must be psychological—maybe I'm just a hypochondriac—that's why I've never told Osman.

The shaking hands are harder to hide. 'How long were you unconscious?'—rummaging through his notes for the answer. (*I was sleeping—didn't set a stop watch.*) 'An appointment with a neurologist might be a good idea. You may have sustained more damage than was obvious initially.'

But the neurologist is busy for the next six weeks. I'll be better by then. Stop the shaking, get co-ordinated; cancel the appointment.

I'm getting better at plastic wrapping. My collar is barely damp after its next shower.

If I don't teach phys ed I could get a job in a sandwich shop. Chief wrapper.

Costa wants Jenny to meet his family some time over the school holidays. Actually Jenny's not sure that 'wants' is the right word—Costa's mum has told him that he has to invite Jenny for lunch.

'I don't think she's going to like me.'

'Everybody likes you! Anyway, relax; you're not marrying the guy.'

Jenny groans, hides her face in a pillow on the floor; I'm sprawled on her bed, the first time I've been to her place since the accident.

'You *are* planning to marry him?'

'I don't know—I don't care about getting married—but I know I'll always want to be with Costa. I can't imagine living without him—we've got so much to say; we talk all the time.'

'All the time?'

'Okay, the other stuff's pretty good too. But I really like him—if I wasn't in love with him I'd still want to be his friend. That's why I want his parents to like me.'

I ask Luke if he's going down to see his dad for Easter. He looks uncomfortable.

'Dad wasn't very happy about my quitting uni, to put it mildly—and my father never puts anything mildly! I just seem to have lost the taste for being constantly reminded what a pathetic loser I am.'

We're still trying for the Happy Family Award, but it doesn't always work. It's like trying to push a pussy pimple back into your forehead—the anger squirts out sideways. Bronwyn spends her life wrapped in bandages and slings; Dad reads the paper as if it's his solemn duty to get worked up over disgusting politicians, and Mum, the lady with the cast-iron constitution, walks around holding her stomach and eats antacid tablets instead of pickled herrings. And me? I just bitch about anything that pops into my head. Anything except what's really wrong.

Dad takes the kids to church Easter Sunday. He took them Good Friday too, and the Sunday before that. We used to be twice-a-year Christians, Christmas and Easter.

Mum decides to have the nursery open all day. She's not impressed with God. 'Look what he did to his own son,' she says. 'Am I supposed to be surprised at what he did to my daughter?'

'It sometimes helps,' says Dad. 'Just being there, sitting quietly.'

I've had enough sitting quietly to last me a lifetime—and I haven't noticed God keeping his side of any bargains lately. They go without me.

The chocolate part of Easter is easier to cope with. Hayden gives me a beautiful egg in a fancy gold box; it's a shame to open it, but I manage.

Luke gives me—and Matt and Bronny—a tiny chocolate bilby. It's too cute to eat.

'Now that you've got the stick,' Luke says, 'you could walk in the bush, couldn't you?'

Mum looks up from her herb encyclopedia and glares at him as if he's suggested Mt Everest.

I wish I'd thought of it myself—I've been so busy hating the stick that I hadn't thought about what it could let me do. And I'm bored and restless after a frustrating day trying to understand a bunch of crap about "Psychological Effects of Stress" . . . 'I might try now—just at the river here.'

'I'll go with you,' Luke says, and Mum relaxes.

Out the back gate—I'm ridiculously excited—and on to the trail by the river. Dad and the kids, walking with Ben, have flattened the long grass from the gate, it's a bit easier than I'd expected, but the trail itself is rougher. Watching for every stick and uneven footstep is exhausting; I have to grab Luke's arm a few times to keep from falling.

I really want to make it to the big log. Hadn't remembered it was so far.

'We're nearly there,' Luke says, gesturing to it before I say anything.

'How'd you know?'

'It's a great log.'

It is. Great to sit on too. *Made it, made it! Feels so good. God, my foot hurts—hope I can make it back.*

'Worth it?' Luke asks.

'Fantastic!'

I still think so three days later when my foot is starting to untwist itself and I can walk around the house again without fighting down a scream.

Maybe that's why I haven't told Hayden about it. I don't know if he'd mind me going with Luke so much as the walk itself.

Finish the neck brace tomorrow, Mr Osman says. No more metal head.

'You're coping with the soft collar for most of the day now?'

'Great.' *Except for the pain, but it's bearable if I spend a few hours lying down. And if I tell him that, I mightn't get rid of the frame.*

'Well then, wear it all day tomorrow, and then start weaning yourself off it. I'll see you again in four weeks—and by then the only thing you should need to wear on your neck is your favourite necklace.'

Now I remember! That's what I was really hanging out for—to wear my pearls again!

Four weeks! Four weeks and I'll be normal. Sometimes I've thought it was never going to happen—but a month I can believe in. Roll on, the 17th of May.

Bare naked neck on my pillow.

Collar when I get up; collar all day till I go to bed. Hotter and scratchier than the brace; gives me a rash, up my throat and down my chest. I can almost nod; I can almost turn my head.

Mum bakes a cake—lemon yoghurt. She'll have to start repeating herself if I get much better.

'What are you going to do with the frame?' Bronwyn asks.

Smash it, squash it, hammer it into little pieces. Melt it down for new coke cans; send it into outer space with the next shuttle.

'It belongs to the hospital,' Dad points out.

'But they'll let us keep it!' Bronny shrieks—nought to full panic in three seconds—'Anna might need it more!'

'I'm not wearing it again! You can take it back today.'

A small silvery monster bursts into the room, beeping shrilly: the frame, covered in foil, with Matthew inside. 'I-am-a-robot!' he chants, in case we haven't guessed.

'Looks much better on you, Matt. You can keep it.'

Costa's parents like Jenny so much that they've asked her to come for dinner after the Easter midnight mass.

How to break it to her that Easter was last week?

'Orthodox Easter,' she explains loftily, 'is calculated differently. It's tomorrow.' Then, promptly switching back from Multicultural Expert of the Week to usual Jenny—'What am I going to wear?'

Just one day without pain. One day being normal again. That's what I'd wish for, if I found the right old lamp. What I could do, in just one day of the old me ... but it's the normal stuff I'd choose—showering standing up, seeing my friends, moaning about problems that don't exist, going to karate, being with Hayden ...

And if the genie did what he was supposed to, two more the same.

For second term I'm going to the first class every day. That'll give me an idea of what's happening so I can follow it up with my tutors. Mum will drop me off, zip over to the nursery for an hour and pick me up after. I don't have to go to Assembly or home room.

It all sounds incredibly artificial. But at least I can do it without my collar.

'Everybody's been asking how you're going,' Jenny says, her voice hardening as she adds, 'except Caroline. So I don't tell her—I wouldn't give her the satisfaction of knowing *anything* about you!'

Mixed in with gardening and cooking books, Mum's got the ones Lynda left. Today she's reading *Stages of Grief, Death and Dying*.

I'm not sure why it makes me so angry. 'I'm not dead, Mum! Not even dying!'

'Dying isn't the only thing to mourn!' she snaps. 'You can deal with things your way, but I'm finding this helpful!'

The mass was amazing, Jenny tells me. The most moving thing she's ever been to. The ornate church, the baritone of the chanting priest, smoking incense in swinging censers—she gets quite poetic in her efforts to make me feel it. 'At five to twelve all the lights went out, to symbolise the death—and at midnight the first candle was lit for the resurrection. It was so dramatic—the flame being passed from candle to candle until everyone in the church was holding a lighted candle and kissing everyone else and saying "*Christos anesti—Alithos anesti*".'

'Sounds very fluent, Jen!'

'It's not hard if you just relax and don't worry about sounding stupid. Anyway . . . when we got back to their house Mrs Mavronas gave us all red-dyed hard boiled eggs—and I got the champion!'

'How do you have a champion *egg*?'

'You smash them against each other and the one that cracks loses—mine squashed all the other eggs before it cracked.'

'You're crazy, Jen.' And not just about Costa; she's fallen in love with everything to do with him.

Term doesn't start till Wednesday, because of Anzac Day. I make it through English, psychology and maths. I'm glad it's a short week.

'It's Mark's eighteenth next Saturday; do you want to come?'

After three months of 'going out' we're actually going *out*! A real live date, like normal people have, not sitting around watching TV with little brothers and sisters.

'Some guys from our school have a band; it should be good.'

We've sparred together but never danced. I mightn't be much good on the fast dances, but slow will be okay, slow will be great—I really want to know how it feels, to be pressed against him with our arms around each other . . .

'Will you have to wear your collar?'

'I don't wear it for fun, you know! I *have* noticed that it's not the perfect fashion accessory!'

'I just asked!'

'Because you're ashamed to be seen with a freak!'

'No! Because—look, I don't need this! Forget it, would you?'

Rerun of our last slamming-door scene—screaming insults he can't hear, wondering whether I want to run after him or never see him again.

I phone Jenny.

'Why is he such a prick, Jen?'

A few months ago she would have said, 'Because he's a man,' but since Costa's appeared, she's become a lot more deep and meaningful. 'I think he's pretty screwed up. He probably feels so guilty about you having to wear the collar that he hates to see you in it.'

'But I'm the one that has to wear it! If I can deal with it, so should he!'

'It's just because he cares about you.'

'I don't know. I don't even know if he meant I should forget about the collar or going to the party. Maybe he means we should forget about us.'

'Just call him. Sort it out—everything will be okay, you'll see.'

Jenny in love, the eternal optimist. Thinks everyone should be as happy as she is.

'I'll talk to you later—I've really got to go now. Costa and I are doing maths.'

'Right. Just try and remember which figures you're supposed to be working on.'

'Spoilsport. Now do what I told you—phone Hayden and sort it out. Promise?'

'I guess so.'

A cup of coffee; a walk around the house. I feel sick; my hands are so sweaty they slip on the buttons. I don't know what I'll do if Hayden dumps me. Everything else in my life is going wrong; I need something stable.

If he doesn't answer himself I'll hang up. Maybe I'll hang up anyway. My voice comes out in such a silly squeak I have to start coughing as an excuse.

'Anna, I'm sorry.'

'I shouldn't have got so upset.'

'I just thought you'd have a better time if you didn't have to wear your collar.'

'Yeah. I'll see. I won't have to wear it forever, you know.'

'I know! Look, I've got to go. I've got a heap of homework. I'll pick you up Saturday, about eight.'

I've worn my collar all day; I had my rest after lunch and I'm resting again after dinner. I'm going to look like a normal person when I go to this party.

Mum comes into my room. 'I know you're nearly eighteen, but—'

(Why is there always a but?)

'—don't forget that anything you drink will be enhanced by your painkillers. And with your balance . . .'

'People will think I'm drunk! Do you think that's the worst thing I've got to worry about?'

'I think falling over and hurting yourself is something to worry about! As well as any girl's . . . the usual problems of losing self-control when you've had too much to drink.'

'Falling into the back seat of Hayden's car in a fit of drunken passion?'

'If you want to put it like that.'

'I don't think you've got anything to worry about. I'll let you know if I get luckier.'

'Very funny. It's just—I know you're sensible, but with all this—I can't help worrying about you.'

'I've noticed.'

Good start to an evening. A patched-up truce with my boyfriend; a nearly-fight with my mother. It's got to improve.

But not by Dad talking to Hayden. 'You're driving?'

'Dad!'

'You can't blame him, Anna.'

Just watch me.

'I'm not trying to be difficult,' Dad goes on, winding himself up to be as difficult as possible, 'but I can remember what it was like to be young—and if it were my best friend's eighteenth, I might have trouble not having a drink. All I'm asking is that if you do, Anna comes home in a taxi.'

'I'll take care of her.'

I don't believe this. What am I, some Jane Austen heroine to be handed over from father to prospective husband? 'Would someone around here give me a little credit for taking care of myself?'

'Of course we do,' chorus the three liars.

I calm down when I'm in the car. No collar, no stick, a boyfriend and a party—tonight I'm nothing but Anna, a normal seventeen-year-old, and I'm going to have normal seventeen-year-old fun. Hayden even decides against explaining why my parents worry about me and starts to relax. He and Mark have been working all day, cleaning out the garage. 'It looks really good,' he says modestly, 'and the band's unbelievable. It's going to be a great night.'

A few people are there already; I give Mark a birthday kiss and present; he tells me I look fantastic and a look that says he means it. I start to believe Hayden: it's going to be a great night. Someone I don't know is coming up to Mark now; Hayden's organising drinks, but Jess from karate has just arrived and I'm really glad to see her, it's been ages. I have to sit down. I find a chair as she comes over.

'I wondered if you'd be here! So are all you better now?'

'Nearly.'

'I heard you were giving up karate.'

'News to me!'

'So why did Hayden quit? I'd heard it was because of you.'

'You heard wrong. I'll be back in a couple of months; Hayden's a big boy—he can make up his own mind.'

'Hey—did you *really* break your neck?'

'*Really*,' I mimic.

'Jeez—you sure were lucky!'

She's bored now; looking around for someone more interesting to talk to. I shouldn't have been such a bitch—I'm not ready to stand up yet. I'll look like an idiot sitting here on my own.

'Have you been to any tournaments lately?' I ask desperately. 'You were doing really well with kata, last time I saw you.'

'Yeah ... Oh look, there's Dave! Catch you later!'

Hayden runs out from behind the bar to bring me a lemon squash. 'Having a good time?'

'I'd rather have a beer. Are you going to be bartender all night?' (*God! I sound so peevish! Try again.*) 'You did a great job on the shed.'

'Thanks. Pasquali's taking over the bar at nine. Here's the band! I was beginning to think they'd got lost.' He rushes over to them and starts lugging black boxes down to the end of the shed.

Legs are working again; there's Jodie; Jodie and Paul, we went to primary school together; go over and see them.

'Anna! Haven't seen you for ages; what've you been up to?'

'Nothing much.' (They don't know! I thought the whole world knew about Anna Duncan's accident. I feel so free!) 'What about you?'

Jodie grins, swinging Paul's hand. 'That'd be telling.'

'I'll get us a drink,' Paul says. 'You want one, Anna?'

'I'd love a beer.' I'm going to have to sit down again before I fall; try and look casual, 'Might as well have a seat, it'll be a while before the band's ready.'

Jodie's wearing white jeans; she glances at the concrete floor. 'No thanks.' Her eyes are already flicking around the room to see who else she knows. Paul arrives with three beers. The band plugs in the amplifier; an electronic screech spears through my head as I reach for my glass and I tip over like a wobbly-doll, pouring beer all over my shirt.

Jodie giggles. 'How much did you have before we got here?'

They wander off. So do I, once my balance trickles back—outside, behind the shed, where I can hide and wring out my sleeve. I'm leaning against the wall crying when Hayden finds me. He puts his arms around me. 'You okay?'

Better now that I'm with him. I press myself against his chest.

'Shit, you're soaked! What happened?'

'It's okay; I just spilled something.'

'We'll see if you can borrow a jumper from Mark's mum.'

I can't argue; I'm too cold and too miserable to even try, and he's dragged me over to the house already. If it wasn't his best friend's party I'd just go home. Mrs Ryan is nice; she doesn't act as if I'm drunk; gives me a red jumper which wouldn't be bad at all if you didn't know that it belonged to your host's mother. I still feel like an idiot. I wish I could stay in this bedroom all night.

'Coming, Anna?' Hayden calls. 'The band's starting. You'll love them.'

'Can you get them to turn it down a bit?' Mark's mum asks. 'It'll be a bit embarrassing if the neighbours ring the police about the noise.'

Hayden tries, but apparently the amplifier doesn't go any lower. The noise rocks the shed; everyone's dancing. Hayden and I shuffle around, not so much dancing as holding. My face is against his chest; he runs his hands down my back till I could melt against him ... I feel dizzy with love.

The song stops. We stay together. The next number starts; fast; it turns into a drum solo. The drum vibrates through me, through my body, through my ears and my brain. It fills my head with blackness and knocks me to the ground.

not fair not fair not fair not fair not fair not fair not fair not fair not fair not fair not fair not fair not fair not fair not fair not fair not fair

CHAPTER 9

Mother's Day. I give Mum *Cakes For Every Day of the Year*. 'Three hundred and sixty-five of them,' I explain. 'You'll be able to celebrate whatever you want.'

'What's the worst?' asks Jenny.

The pain in my neck. No; the foot's sharper. The ringing in my ears; the dizziness. The shaking, the spilling drinks, slobbering food. The not being able to do anything . . . Hayden not kissing me . . . The way it all doesn't stop. *Why doesn't it stop?*

'Everything. I'm pissed off, Jen. I've had it.'

For English this week Martin's set me two chapters to study and a poem to write. 'Try writing a poem that expresses how you feel about yourself,' he says. 'Show us the real you.'

The real me? Fifteen weeks ago I might have known who she was—now I'm a mask and don't know whether I'm more scared of looking under it or letting other people know I'm afraid.

But he wants a poem and he wants it deep and meaningful.

Peeling like an onion,
I am shedding filmy layers
the firm white flesh revealing
what's hidden deep inside.

Opening like a babushka
I am sorting wooden dolls
the last hollow doll is holding
the baby deep inside.

Unwrapping like a present
I am crumpling pretty papers
under the crepe and ribbons
there's a perfect gift inside.

Which is a lie from one end to the other but might keep Martin happy.

'You know the stuff we're doing on motivation in psych,' Jenny begins—but I'm still on stress, and it's bull.

She ignores that. 'It's really got me in ... you can apply it to people you know and things start to make sense.'

'Like your friend going crazy because she broke her neck?'

'Idiot! You're not crazy. I was thinking about Caroline—I had to try and get my head around how she could dump you like that ... and why I hate her so badly now. I know she was mean to you and broke up our friendship—but I really *hate* her. Worse than you do.'

God, I'm a selfish bitch. It's never struck me before that Jenny lost a friend too. 'And?'

'I figure I feel a bit guilty.'

'How could you feel guilty? I couldn't have made it through all this if you hadn't stuck around!'

'You would have—but thanks. Anyway, I was reading this thing about survivor guilt and it was so cool! It just exactly described the way I feel.'

'If you were a real friend you'd have broken your neck too?'

'Something like that.'

'Bad idea. So you figure Caroline's so competitive she'd have to go one step better and actually kill herself to still be my friend?'

Jenny laughs. 'I hadn't thought of that one. But I still think it's something to do with being competitive—you know how good she was to you in hospital?'

'Now you're trying to make me feel guilty—all those little presents.'

'As if she had to be the best at being a best friend!'

And if I'm really honest, did it work? Did part of me think that she cared more about me because of the strawberries and talcum powder?

'But it would have been a terrible strain to keep it going; she's too much of a perfectionist to just slack off, so she had to drop you completely.'

'I thought maybe it was because I was messy—I broke the rule about getting better when I left hospital.'

'That too—and maybe it was safer to blame you for not being well, because if it wasn't your fault, then it could happen to anyone—even perfectionists.'

Mum and her new cookbook have come up with a mocha cake in a ring. 'It looks like your collar!' Bronny says.

'Cut it up!' Matt shrieks, getting into the spirit, and Mum smiles.

'You didn't think I'd miss celebrating the end of your collar, did you?'

Mr Osman is admiring my nude neck. *Oops—forgot my pearls.*

'Still having any pain?'

'Not when I'm lying down.'

'We might X-ray it again to check the healing's all gone as it should.'

Too bad—you got this far, and now your head's going to fall off.

'And your physio's not very happy with that ankle.'

I've noticed. As if forcing a stick onto me isn't enough, he's started muttering about balance and equilibrium and the fact that mine are stuffed. I'm just hanging out for when I can really get into the exercises. The left ankle's finally gone back into a normal shape and is starting to move, but the right one still looks like a puffer fish. If I can get them both going everything will be okay.

Mr Osman wants to see the right one perform. It goes through its version of up/down, round and round; the movements are so small it's hard to tell which one it's trying. Mr Osman grabs it and tries to show it what to do. The bones in my heel screech and grate, but they're stronger than he is. It doesn't move.

'Better X-ray that foot at the same time,' he decides.

'I've decided,' Jenny announces. 'I'm going to do Psychology next year.' She's waiting for me to say something rude, but it's her life.

Besides, her theories about Caroline almost make sense.

Going out after maths to meet Mum, my heart lurches with surprise. It's not Mum, it's Luke leaning against the car, waiting for me. For just a moment the background fades—administration wing, car park, trees and football oval all disappear, and I can't see anything except a man with a long dark ponytail and changeable blue eyes, watching for me as if there's nothing in the world that could be more important than this.

Funny how when you see somebody out of context everything looks different, as if they're a stranger you're meeting for the first time. How you suddenly notice that the body you always thought of as just average is actually lean and fit and downright hunky, that the grin when he sees you is incredibly sexy . . . or would be if you didn't know him so well, and you didn't already have a boyfriend.

But it still makes leaving school after first class seem like an adventure instead of a wimp-out.

'Your mum couldn't get away—you don't mind?'

'I'll cope.' And the breathlessness goes away; it's okay, it's only Luke, my friend. It's just the first time I've realised what a good friend he's become.

'You dying to get home or do you want to stop for a cappuccino?'

'In my school uniform?'

'You're right; it's too risky. Imagine the headline: Cappuccino Caper—Girl Swaps Calculus for Coffee.'

I laugh, but there's a niggle of truth in his teasing, and once we're at the table and I'm licking the chocolaty froth off my spoon he adds sternly, 'If you're too sick to be at school you'll stay in your bedroom and feel miserable!'

Flick a bit of froth at him. 'My dad doesn't sound like that!'

'No—that was mine, scaled down for cafe volume. So what's your excuse for being afraid to enjoy yourself?'

'I'm not!'

'That's true. I should have said too angry.'

'It's just so frustrating! One class and I'm stuffed.'

The good thing about Luke is that he doesn't remind me that a month ago I couldn't have sat through even one class. I *know* that—but I still want to be better now. 'It's a bummer,' he says. 'Sometimes I wonder how I'd deal with it, if it were me.'

'You'd be fine! Sit and philosophise your way out of it.'

'Wouldn't be that easy if I were the one hurting. I'd like to think I'd be as strong as you, but I don't know.'

Take a long sip of my coffee. It's the steam that's making my eyes water.

'It's a little out of alignment,' Mr Osman says, studying my new neck X-rays, 'the damaged vertebra is sitting forward on the one below it—but I think it's stable. It shouldn't cause any real problems.'

This is my neck, my spinal cord—I want guarantees, not shoulds.

'What about the pain?' Mum asks sharply. 'That seems a very real problem to me—Anna's in terrible pain most of the time. Shouldn't that have improved by now?'

Early days, he mutters; these things take time, can't rush the body's healing processes.

He might be a brilliant surgeon but he's not too hot on counting. Three and a half months by my reckoning.

'What'd he say about your foot?' Jenny asks when she's run out of original names for arrogant bastards.

'Long names and bad news. Then gave me a lecture about doing my exercises and not just expecting the physio to work magic.'

Shrieks from the other end of the phone. 'Did you tell him you're the world's worst exercise fanatic?'

'I think he got the idea when Mum tried to strangle him.'

'I would have helped her.'

Now I know what the worst thing is. It's being angry. It's being so angry that I can't even see, and not being able to do anything about it. Can't jog, can't slam my punching bag, can't exercise till I drop. Nothing to do with my rage but choke it down inside, where it bubbles and swells till I'm afraid I'll drown in my own boiling lava.

Time is racing and I'm standing still. The term's slipping away—Year 12, the most important year of my life, nearly half gone and I've barely started it yet, sitting in class for an hour a day—the only thing I'm taking in is that every day I'm a little further behind.

Which is why Mr Sandberg's 'dropped in' after school again—suddenly it's only four weeks till mid-year exams. Two fortnights. There's no way I'll be ready.

'We can defer if we have to,' he says. 'But realistically . . . have you thought any more about doing it over two years?'

'You'd have a better chance of getting the marks you want,' Mum adds, but what she means, what they both mean, is that it's better than failing, and that's what I'm doing now.

I can't shout at Mr Sandberg but I don't have to stick around and be insulted. 'I'll think about it.'

But he's a teacher—he gets the last word as I stomp off to my room. 'Think about it soon, Anna! We're running out of time.'

Hayden and I are perched on stools at the counter of the Pizza Palace. It takes all my concentration to balance but that's okay, I'm doing it, I'm not falling off. After Mark's party I thought he might never be game to take me out again, and I'm not going to blow it.

'What's the walking stick for?' asks the waitress.

My song and dance routine! 'I hurt my foot,' I mutter.

'That's a shame! Never mind—it's just will power, isn't it? Think positive and you'll get there!'

'You know what I want for my birthday?' I ask Hayden after she's gone, and the poor guy looks relieved—he must have been afraid I was going to hit her. He's probably right, except I would have fallen off the stool. 'An electric cattle prod.'

He's not looking relieved after all. I think embarrassed is the word—or apprehensive.

'Just a little zap for people who ask if I hurt myself at netball and tell me I'll be right,' I add.

'Calm down,' Hayden pleads, but I go on with my hate list.

'Three zaps for stories about one-armed swimmers, and ten for the next person who tells me about someone dying of cancer right after they broke their ankle!'

'They're just trying to help,' Hayden says, and asks if we can have a table with proper chairs. I want to say we'll stay on the stools, but balancing has just gobbled up my quota of positive thinking for the day.

'Always someone worse off than you,' I remember later. That's the worst of all. Am I supposed to be happy that orphans in Bosnia have had their legs blown off? To not mind my pain because other people can't buy painkillers? I don't want things like this to happen to *anyone*; the images of torn-apart children, raped women and murdered men pile on top of me in a suffocating mass of grey.

That's when I understand Jenny's survivor guilt—my brand is not-the-very-worst-victim guilt. As if I shouldn't complain about walking badly when some people can't walk at all.

A hundred zaps for that.

I'm glad I wasn't around when Dad phoned Osman; nothing more embarrassing than watching your parents make a scene. It's been bad enough watching him rant and rave around the house, working up to it.

So Mr Osman decided that perhaps it would be worth doing CT and bone scans of both neck and ankle—anything to shut my father up. And since they have to be done in Melbourne, his secretary even arranged for appointments the same day as I go down to see the neurologist. *A day of non-stop fun: father and daughter quality time.*

Half an hour in the car and I wish I still had my collar . . . an hour and I'd have worn the frame . . . two hours and we're there but my neck hurts so much I can hardly walk from the carpark to the hospital. I'm injected with radioactivity; relieved to find I don't glow; back to the coffee shop for milkshake and painkillers while I wait for the dye to spread through my bones.

Not much to do in a hospital waiting room. Dad and I wander around the gift shop; I buy a Cosmo; he plays with a whirling bouncy spring-thing and buys it for Matt—then has to look for something for Bronny. This is the perfect place to shop for a child hypochondriac; we finally choose a stethoscope that the package claims 'really works' and costs five times as much as the spring.

'You've got to be fair. I think she feels a bit left out.'

'What do I get?'

'A day out in the big city.'

'Next time you can take the kids and I'll have the spring-thing.'

Finally it's time to go back upstairs; the lift makes me stagger, and Dad takes my arm. I would really hate to throw up in a lift.

'Lie still,' the technician says, as I slide into the CT's coffin-womb; he doesn't know how good it feels to lie down— I'll be as still as he likes if he lets me stay on this bed. Ankles, then neck; then across the hall to another hard bed, a machine looming over me and a monitor with tiny pictures of white bones.

'Do you have much pain in your left ankle?' he asks.

'Not as much as the right.'

'You've had a fair bit of damage in it too!' he says sharply. 'Was it never X-rayed?'

Bonus! Two arthritic ankles instead of one! But I feel a dark swirl of pleasure—I wasn't being a wimp when I said that ankle hurt too.

A sandwich and another drink and on to the neurologist. If Dad gets any more stressed with Melbourne traffic and finding a parking place he'll be the one needing a doctor.

Unfortunately it's still me the secretary calls, and me that the doctor tells to strip down to bra and pants.

And it's no good telling myself that they're just the same as bathers—nobody else is going swimming.

He taps, finds reflexes, plays a guessing game of pricking me with pins or dabbing with cotton wool. Tells me I can get dressed and watches my hands shake as I do up my buttons. I'm starting to sway; he gives me a chair. Touch his finger, touch my nose. Well, nearly. Try again. Who wants to touch their nose anyway?

'Stand up; close your eyes.'

Stand up; get kicked in the head by invisible van Damme; fall down flat. Speedy reflexes are what make a good neurologist; he catches me before I hit the floor.

'Try again. I won't let you fall.'

It's so simple. Of course I can do it. Stand up and close my eyes—everyone can do that.

Everyone but me. Close my eyes; fall; doctor catches me. Sickest game I've ever played. Luckily he gets tired of it before I show him exactly how sick.

'How do you feel?'

Room spinning, legs wobbling . . . 'Not great.'

'Nasty sort of bloke, aren't I? We'll call your dad in to talk about it.'

He has a kind face and looks sorry for me. That's almost worse than Osman's callousness. He gets out a diagram and Dad looks studious; some problems . . . cerebellar signs . . . but it's still early in terms of recovery, and I'm young . . .

The words float over me. The brain he's discussing has left the room, is drifting somewhere in the grey sky outside the window.

On the way home pain fills the car like mist; I wonder how Dad can see through it to drive. Half way he says we'll stop for a drink. It's a long walk across the footpath and into the cafe. Dad's looking worried; he helps me to a chair and goes up to order.

The pain is creeping up from my neck, over my head, through my brain, blocking everything on its way. I hold my head between my hands, resting on the table. The cafe is dark; is black. I slump forward onto the table just as Dad slides a jelly slice in front of me.

I can see again. Dad's holding my shoulders, propping me up in the chair. The jelly slice is smashed. Raspberry; my favourite. The shop owner is rushing across with a glass of water; the cafe is very quiet, everyone staring at the girl who can't remember how to sit up.

'I'm all right.'

I drink the water to prove it, and start to feel a little better.

Dad and the shop owner help me out to the car, like a protester being escorted off the premises by police. Dad wants to take me to a doctor, but I've seen enough of them for one day. I talk him into taking me straight home to hide in my own bed.

Sadness is grey, despair matt black and anger blood red. Bitterness is almost beautiful, like an iridescent poisonous bug—shiny black shot through with a deep, reddy purple.

Jenny's planning again. 'Why don't you and Hayden come to the production with Costa and me? It's *Oliver*—I've heard the rehearsals and it sounds great.'

Because I don't want to leave the house; because this deep feeling about knowing I'm supposed to be with Hayden doesn't translate into us ever having a good time together; because I just don't feel like watching a bunch of pretend orphans dance and sing while a drunk murders a prostitute.

Poor Jen. She hasn't had much luck talking me into anything lately. Shopping, clothes, hair; she wants me to experiment, play the game—but they just don't seem important any more.

'I know how much your foot hurts,' she says, trying to convince me to wear my mini skirt for out-of-uniform day, 'but at least your legs still *look* great. And you're so slim! Wish I had your willpower.'

I don't know if I still have willpower. The next doctor I see will probably find that's been damaged too.

Then she wants to braid my hair. 'You've had it just tied back for ages'—*since Mum combed the glass out in hospital*—'don't you want to try something fancier?'

Braiding was for karate. And it takes too long—I can't be bothered. Jenny tries a few different ways of pulling it back and tying it up, but the next day I can't remember which one she said looked good, and yank it into an elastic again.

She can't be having fun, being with me. She's lively and bubbly; she needs a friend who's alive. She's just being kind.

I'm running to answer the phone. Quickly, smoothly—perfect symmetrical steps springing off the balls of my feet. Running like an athlete.

'You idiot!' I tell myself. 'You could do it all along—you were just too scared to try.'

A ray of hope makes my whole day glow, though I can't remember why. Must be a sign I'm getting better.

The phone rings; I leap up instinctively and try to run—my ankle gives way and knocks me to the ground. I remember the dream as I stagger up and across the room in my usual hobble—right foot dragging, everything hurting.

I reach the phone as it goes dead.

If I thought life was going to go on being like this forever I couldn't take it. *Wouldn't* take it. No one could make me.

CHAPTER 10

I'm in Mr Osman's rooms again, with the damning evidence of scans held up against the light.

'. . . never walk on rough ground again.' That's what the CT pictures tell him. *What are they, a crystal ball?*

But I don't say anything so witty; I sit there stunned. 'Never' is such a big word; a cold word, when you put it with an everyday verb like 'walk'; a gigantic carved lump of silver ice. *Never never never never.*

He's using it again; this time for high heels.

I didn't think I'd care about that, but I do—I want to choose. If the pain gets worse—*worse? There's worse?*—I can have my foot fused; frozen, so it doesn't move at all. *Worse, worser and worst.* The best thing for now will be a splint, some kind of orthotic device. *Worster—infinite worses.* Now I've got rid of the neck brace I can wear leg irons.

I find my voice at last, though it comes out in a squeak. 'But you said it was just sprained!' I'm not going to be able to finish the sentence without crying—*sprained ankles get better.*

He blusters a bit. The first X-rays didn't show the extent of the damage, sometimes these things are hard to pick. But my broken vertebra definitely seems quite stable, he adds cheerfully. Still in the wrong place, but not likely to snap again and kill me.

That's really something to celebrate, now that I'm crippled for life.

I wonder if Bronny has any spare dolls. Do you have to be a witch doctor to voodoo, or can anyone do it?

I wake in the night with all the questions I was too stunned to ask. How much pain is 'some'? How rough is rough ground? Has Mr Osman ever heard that bones belong to people—and what does 'can't' mean anyway?

And the one creeping through every thought, the one I smash back every time I see it: can I still do karate—or phys ed?

And if not, will I still be me?

Jenny's having concentration problems too. Just over a week till exams and she still can't go for more than thirty seconds without thinking about Costa. Her parents have put a fifteen-minute limit on phone calls but that doesn't guarantee what she thinks about when she hangs up.

'Sometimes I think it'd be better if we actually slept together. Maybe then I wouldn't think about him all the time.'

I stop doing my balancing exercises for a moment—it seems a bit insensitive to practise standing on one leg when your friend's talking about stuff like this. 'Sounds like a drastic solution . . . mightn't it work the other way?'

'Probably—I was just joking, anyway!'

'It didn't sound like it.'

'I'm not ready for that kind of commitment.'

'So tell him! Don't let him pressure you.'

'He's not—it's me; I never thought I'd want to so much! I mean, he wants to—half the time I think he'd do it in the hall between classes if I suggested it—did I tell you about Chris and Brad?'

'They're not together, are they?'

'Very together when her dad caught them! They snuck back to her place at lunchtime, and guess who came home for a sandwich . . .'

'God, how awful!' I'm laughing so hard Mum comes in from the lounge to see what's wrong and I have to wave her away—but I can't help feeling sorry for Chris.

'Would kind of put you off, wouldn't it? I figure that's why Costa doesn't mind waiting—he wants it to be so good we'll just have to keep on going—and that's what I'm afraid of. I really love him, I already love him so much—if I sleep with him I feel like it'll be total—there'll be no escape, that's it—we'll be together forever.'

'I thought that was what you wanted?'

'It is! Just not yet. Sometimes I wish that I hadn't met him yet! Why couldn't I have had this year with lots of fun, go out with a bunch of different guys, no commitment—and then met Costa and fallen in love?'

'Life is tough!'

'Sorry. I'm a great friend, whingeing about finding the perfect guy too soon, when you've got real problems.'

'That's okay—I'm sick of mine. Yours are more interesting.'

'Maybe ... but I couldn't tell them to anyone except you! My dad's going to hang up if I don't say goodbye—back to the grindstone.'

In the honesty of my bed at night I know I've never felt anything like what Jenny's going through. Loving someone so much it threatens to take you over, what's the saying? ... consuming passion; being eaten up by love. No wonder she sometimes gets scared; don't know if I'd like it.

But part of me can't help being jealous. How can Hayden and I ever get something going when he's still terrified that I'll break if he touches me?

'What have you decided?' Mr Sandberg asks.

'Martin thinks I'll be ready to do the English exam.' *If you really work*, he'd said; *focus just on this one subject—not sounding convinced, but seeing how desperate I am to accomplish something.*

'It'll be a massive amount of work if you defer everything to second semester. I need an answer for exactly what you're going to do by the start of next term.'

'You'll get it!'

Shouting would have earned a detention before, but now all I get is a raised eyebrow.

But I've made one decision, that'll do for today—I'll worry about the rest after the exam. Lisa agrees, when she's finished telling me that Becky can roll over—both ways! Throw everything into English and see what happens.

What happens is that I'm sure I've passed. Not brilliantly; ran out of time to finish the last essay, but I should have made a C; won't think any higher ... but maybe, maybe a B.

Luke picks me up afterwards; takes me home; makes me a cup of coffee and a sandwich. I tell him I can do it, but he knows me too well, knows I'm too tired and sore to bother.

'Your neck's really hurting, isn't it? Do you want a massage?'

He stands behind my chair, rubbing my neck up into where the muscles are screaming at the base of my skull, around on the aching shoulders and their tender blades. The tightness begins to melt. Feels good, so good ... 'You don't have anything else to do today, do you? Maybe you could do this all afternoon.'

'I can think of worse fates.' But he does stop, eventually, when I've drifted into a relaxed glow, dreamier than sleep. I'm still half in it as I get up to see him go.

And kiss him, I don't know why, it seems the right thing to do—a thankyou kiss—except it's so sweet, so good, pulling feelings from so far down inside me, and he holds me so tight and so long that I feel our bodies memorising each other—*this is where I belong, this is where I want to be!*—and when he leaves neither of us speaks.

'What did you think of the exam?'

Hayden's voice on the phone gives me a jolt of surprise; I haven't thought of him all day. Almost of disappointment; almost thinking that Luke might ring to say—what?

There's nothing to say. Just a kiss between friends. No tongues, no hands, just a kiss. Doesn't mean anything. Nothing to feel guilty about.

Hospital Mourns Distinguished Surgeon, the local rag announces in black type on the front page: Mr Osman is dead. He had a heart attack on Saturday in the middle of a squash game.

I shouldn't have thought about voodoo dolls.

I read on. He was playing with another doctor (gorgeous Alex?) who was unable to revive him. He was rushed to the hospital and pronounced dead on arrival.

Did he have time to notice the pain? To think, 'So that's why people don't like it!'—and a little stinging regret that he hadn't been nicer?

My doctor's dead. That wasn't the way I thought it happened.

But there's still a whole galaxy of other doctors the neurologist wanted me to see—doctors I've never heard of, a different doctor for every different part of me—so we're off to Melbourne for the school holidays. Aunt Lynda lives in Brunswick, in a tiny terrace house—two bedrooms, a lounge room and kitchen all lined up in a row with a narrow hall down the side and the bathroom and laundry tacked on as an afterthought. But she insists that there's plenty of room for Mum, the kids and me—Dad's glued to his office by Tax Time—and that we aren't putting her out at all. Nothing she likes better than an extra four people for ten days of doctors' appointments, and she's taken a week off to prove it.

This morning she's taking Bronny and Matt to the zoo while Mum and I set off to the first waiting room.

The secretary calls my name; I get ready to be a monkey.

Lynda says she didn't think so many people would want to go to the zoo in the pouring rain. She says it's surprising how rain enhances rather than washes away certain smells. She says she always thought she had a dirty mind, but she was streets behind the monkeys. Matt starts to demonstrate what she's talking about, and she reminds him about the ice cream-bribe not to. Matt thought that was just for the zoo.

Mum asks Bronwyn what she liked best.

The Butterfly House, and she's brought me one in her pocket, since I couldn't go. 'It was dead already! Someone would have stepped on it.'

Lynda remembers why she didn't have children.

Doctors, therapists, technicians, tests on part of me I didn't know I had—I know more than any careers officer about all the different health professions. I stagger from one to the other, answering the same questions, telling the same story until it blurs with the tests, the good advice and bad news, into one fortnight-long nightmare. I learn interesting facts but not what to do with them.

The ringing in my ears is called tinnitus; it might go away or it mightn't. Neck pain sometimes gets better and sometimes doesn't; nobody knows why. My hearing's not that bad; if I can't follow a conversation the problem is more likely cognitive than hearing. *Cognitive means thinking—I'm still smart enough to know that.* I feel slapped. That's what I get for admitting the truth, for once.

I still can't do the standing-up, closing-my-eyes trick and if it's a small doctor with slow reflexes I can knock him flying.

But there's nothing wrong with my eyes, I can see the chart on the wall; can find the pinpricks of moving light on the black screen in front of me. The only reason I bump into everything is that looking around makes me dizzy, so my brain tells my eyes not to bother.

I also get dizzy when I'm shut in a small dark cupboard and spun around and around in a chair. And when hot water is pumped into my ears I'm so dizzy I throw up. 'I don't think you'll ever be a sailor,' the technician says, mopping up the floor, the bed, her sleeve, 'you certainly do get dizzy!'

Thank God for science. I might never have noticed.

She gives me a page of eye exercises that might help. 'You don't need to wrap yourself up in cotton wool,' she says, 'just don't do anything silly—like crossing the street by yourself.'

Luckily she doesn't say it in front of Mum.

Lynda gives me mint tea to help my nausea.

'I grow herbs,' Mum says, 'I don't drink them.' She opens a bottle of wine.

When the doctors say my vertebrae are stable it doesn't actually mean safe. No skiing, no horseback riding or contact sports—but a pretty girl like me would hardly be into boxing, would she? And if I go to a gym don't use a punching bag or work out with weights. Or use a hammer or a lawn mower; that could be bad. Nobody says exactly what 'bad' means. I don't think I know what anything means.

People that make splints are called orthotists; 'Orthotics and prosthetics,' the guy explains, sliding the white plastic monstrosity into my shoe, telling me no one will notice the three centimetres sticking up over the edges, 'orthotic insoles, artificial limbs, all that sort of thing.' I picture storerooms full of artificial legs, hands, breasts? . . .

'They'd send you to a psychiatrist if they thought you were crazy,' Lynda says, making everyone a calming chamomile tea for breakfast. 'The neuropsychologist will just be checking for brain damage.'

Thanks, Lynda. Very reassuring.

Mum's anxious to get going. She needs a detour into Rathdowne Street for a morning *caffe latte*.

'I'll go mad if Lynda makes me any healthier,' she explains, adding an espresso to prove it.

My mum the addict.

For the neuropsychologist I don't have to undress—she just peels away my mind, asking about my memory, my concentration, my paying attention, what kind of student was I before?

If I had to choose my own sessions of hell, I'd take naked body over naked brain. Naked body you've still got somewhere left to hide, but this is it, nowhere left to go—this is Anna, all pinned out on the dissection bench.

Commonsense questions; general knowledge—so far so good. She tells me a story and I tell it back. Kindergarten games, getting harder, designed to trick, to make you feel worse when you bomb out. Lists of words, books of pictures—choose the ones you've seen before. The words are easy; the pictures impossible.

Lists of numbers, to add and remember and add again but I've forgotten which one I'm remembering, which one I need and which one to forget, I can't even add the numbers, 'nine and six are fourteen,' I say, it doesn't sound right but by then she's said two more numbers, slippery ones, they slide through my mind, through the blackness and I hold my head in my hands to stop the swaying. 'Sixteen,' I say—it's a good number, as good as any—and hear her close the book. And sigh.

'Well, Anna,' she says at last, 'I think we're starting to see a pattern here. The brain is an extraordinarily complex machine, and when it's injured . . . '

. . . it can shut down so it doesn't have to hear anything it doesn't want to.

Maybe I should care about this poor little brain, this sad, damaged little brain, but it doesn't seem to matter. Nothing seems to matter except sleep; I just want to let myself sink into the woolly blackness and never wake up.

Mum and Dad say I've slept for three days, that's enough. They say I have to get up and go to school, as if one class a day could make any difference to my life.

I'll get up tomorrow. Today I need to sleep.

'You win!' I shout at Mr Sandberg, 'I'll drop everything except English and maths till next year.'

'Let's hope your attitude improves by then,' he snaps, but still lets me slam out of his room without a detention.

Home and back to bed.

Mum and Dad are wide awake and arranging a nightmare: a pow-wow with all the chiefs and the killing reports to decide what to do about me. They've been phoning the insurance officer, phoning doctors, phoning teachers, phoning therapists. Busy busy busy. I wonder if Mum will bake a devil's food cake to celebrate this particular hell.

I want my life back. I want to be me, the way I was the morning we set off for the tournament, five and a half months ago.

Now mornings are black. I lie very still and pretend I'm still asleep. The day stretches out in infinite bleakness—when I move the pain will start. My bed is kind; it doesn't expect anything of me.

'Anna!' Matt shrieks. 'Your boyfriend's here! Do you want him to come in and play? How come you're still in bed anyway? It's nearly teatime.'

'I'll be there in a second.'

I look awful. Pull on jeans and a jumper, brush my hair—don't look much better. Feel worse.

Hayden's standing back, looking stiff and unnatural. 'You want to go for coffee?'

Shouldn't my heart lurch at the sound of his voice? Shouldn't I want him to hold me tight against him till the cold lump of ice inside has melted and I'm me again?

'Are you going to tell me what I've done?' he asks, starting the car, 'or you going on with this silent treatment?' Not tender, not angry, just matter of fact.

Can't you see there's nothing in me to say? Misery seeps through me like black tears, like the radioactive dye, through bones and hair and soul. When the car stops my hand is on the doorhandle, but I can't remember what I'm supposed to do with it. Hayden says something—teasing? teaching?—the words are blurred as jelly on a hot day. Then the metal latch reminds my hand what to do, my legs remember how to get out, how to walk into the cafe, and my body follows. Going out with my boyfriend. I dig up a smile, and paste it on my face.

'I know you've got problems,' Hayden is saying, 'do I know you've got problems! But you're not the only one with feelings.'

We're back at the house, he's leaving and I should call him back, if I can just explain everything will be okay.

But the swirling fog of my brain is whirling too hard and too black, wiping away caring, wiping away sorry, and when it's wiped the blackboard clean I see the words written and know that Hayden is better off without me because my life has already ended. And Luke—why did I kiss Luke? Don't want to think about it, it's too hard, too much; I can't understand anything any more except that there's no way out.

I say I'm asleep when Hayden phones, tell Jenny I can't talk, tell Luke I'm going straight in to study when he drives me home from school.

There's a letter from the insurance people on my father's desk. The words leap out at me: **permanently impaired.**

Which word is worse, permanent or impaired?

Impaired's an ugly word. Worse than handicapped. Disabled. Invalid.

Am I disabled?

How could I be? I'm still the same person—just can't do a few things—like walk much, or stand up for more than a minute, or sit for too long, or . . .

When do you stop being normal and turn into a handicapped person?

You'd have to know it if you were disabled. Wouldn't you?

'Invalid' is a funny word. You say it one way it means a sick person. 'Enfeebled,' says the dictionary, 'or disabled by illness or injury.'

Say it another way and it means not true. Not valid. Worthless.

Why didn't my neck go back that extra fraction of a millimetre? Why the freak chance that stopped it just short of snapping the cord? It would have been so much simpler.

Everyone would have been sad, but they'd have got over it. Matt wouldn't be such a ratbag. Bronny wouldn't be such a hypochondriac. Mum wouldn't have an ulcer and Dad would be his normal placid self; Jenny and Caroline would still be friends. Hayden might feel guilty, but there'd be nothing to remind him all the time; he'd be okay by now too. Luke would have found a decent job. They'd have all been much better off without me.

Six months was the deal, God. You haven't got long left to keep your side of the bargain.

Our lounge room is overflowing with grim people with grimmer reports. Mum and Dad, Mr Sandberg, the insurance officer, Brian the physio, Julie the OT, the two tutors, and Dr Fuller, our GP, who's carrying a foot-high file of reports.

Hairy Legs the insurance officer is running the meeting; she wants to get started. We're all here, she says, for one reason. 'We all want the best for Anna. Now the purpose of coming together tonight is to pool our information to help Anna and her parents plan a suitable treatment and school program for both the immediate and medium-range future.'

Dr Fuller offers to start by summarising the reports from the various specialists I've visited. Heavy grey sounds, words carved on slugs of lead, thump past our heads. Vestibular disturbance, cerebellar symptoms, attention deficit, short-term memory, concentration, sympathetic nervous system, subtalar disruption, traumatic spondylisthesis, chronic pain ... Like blood-filled water balloons, the words burst and seep across the cream Berber carpet.

A minute's silence as he finishes the last report. 'Well,' says Mr Sandberg, 'that sounds like enough to be going on with!'

Hairy Legs is not amused.

Physio Brian talks about the new type of exercises he's worked out for me. He's still hopeful, he says. He wants to continue seeing me twice a week.

OT Julie says that my thumb appears to have stabilised but that she'd like to do another home visit and school visit. She mentions aids and adaptations, posture and ergonomics, computer and tape recorder alternatives to my shaky writing; maybe a visit to the Independent Living Centre.

That's what Caroline meant about special treatment! Poor Caroline, having hands that don't shake.

Mr Sandberg asks if I have a lawyer. Hairy Legs says this is not the appropriate time to discuss legal questions. As the insurance company's representative she will ensure that I receive everything I'm entitled to.

Mr Sandberg looks sceptical.

'The most important thing to decide right now,' Dad says, taking charge, 'is schooling.'

'I decided last week,' I interrupt. 'I'm finishing English and maths and doing the rest next year.'

'You could have told us!' Mum snaps; even Dad lets the mask drop for a minute and looks hurt—humiliated in front of the crowd.

'I forgot.' Nobody understands that none of this matters, it's just a going-through the motions, if you don't exist behind your body then it doesn't matter if you finish Year 12 in one year or twenty.

'Any plans for what you want to do?' Dr Fuller asks.

'Teach phys ed.'

I'm not stupid. I know what their faces will say to that. No one's got the nerve to say it out loud.

They've got the nerve for one more thing, though. 'Is Anna seeing a psychologist?' Julie asks, avoiding my eye.

'If Dr Fuller feels it's appropriate,' says Hairy Legs, 'the insurance will cover it.'

I can't stay quiet any longer. 'You think talking to someone is going to make me feel better about this? My body's wrecked, my life's screwed—I am NOT going to see a psychologist!'

You can dissect my body, my brain, on the coffee table with the tea and banana cake, but you can get out of my mind, that last little inner bit of me, Anna me.

CHAPTER 11

It's been the coldest July on record. The coldest, the wettest, the greyest, though the weatherman doesn't measure grey. August looks as though it'll be the same—Mum complains that her bulbs are late; on the river side of the fence the wattles can't be bothered to bloom.

Cold and bleak, inside and out.

I can't hibernate forever. I'm floating through the world in a mist, on the wrong side of a glass barrier; I can see people but not touch them. School friends keep it light and breezy, their eyes twitching past me; tutors keep it light and easy, a little work and a little chat—Martin's writing a book, Baby Becky can sit up. Mum and Dad, Bronny and Matt, Hayden, Jenny, and Luke—they haven't given up on me and sometimes I think I could reach them if could just remember how to try.

Three weeks till my birthday—the birthday I wasn't going to have unless I was better. I haven't changed my mind. I've put up with this for six months now; I don't see how anyone can expect more than that.

Jenny comes around with a stack of books from her mum: self-healing; do-it-yourself miracles. I flip through the first one: meditation; understanding your motives for not being well—*motives*? What kind of motive could you have for pain?

'Everything that happens, happens for a reason,' I read. 'Nothing is an accident.'

So what the hell would you call it?

> If you are injured by a car racing through a red light, you must ask yourself why you planned to be at that intersection at that time? You will have had a reason for arranging that meeting and choosing the particular injuries or illnesses that resulted. Only when you find that reason will you be able to heal yourself.

I feel like throwing up—preferably on the book. 'Crap! What complete and utter crap!' How could I have willed Hayden to drive at exactly the speed he did so that we'd get to that intersection at exactly the same second as Trevor Jones—let alone how I went about willing a dickhead I'd never met to drive down a road I'd never noticed. It's too stupid to think about. But I can't stop myself from reading a bit more.

> Even children who are abused by their parents have made that decision, when as free souls they chose parents whom they knew would abuse them. For the soul is wise and chooses the life that will teach it the most on each stage of its journey.

Worse than stupid—evil. The sickest thing I've heard since the neo-Nazis tried to claim the Holocaust was a myth. It's not only okay for Trevor Jones to slam into me and ruin my life, it's even okay for parents to torture their children, because that's what the children chose as an interesting lesson! In fact whatever horrendous thing you want to do to anyone else must be okay, because their soul planned for you to do it, no matter what their body thought. According to this wanker.

I'd have never made a bulimic—I can't throw up on command. But there's always another solution. It's not a very big book; more of a fat pamphlet. I shred it into tiny pieces and flush it down the toilet.

The world is so empty. Too drained for anger. I'm hollow inside, except for the tears. They ooze out when I don't expect them; ooze like mud, muddy misery.

Hayden and I are sitting together on the sofa, not quite touching and nothing to say, watching a holiday program with my family. The presenters are sailing the Whitsundays in a charter yacht; after the break they'll have a go at rock climbing in the Grampians.

No one else is crying.

How can I even know who I am when I can't do anything?

Jen won't give up on me either. Now she wants me to try and tell her exactly what's wrong. *My life, basically. Too much to think about.* But she keeps on pushing till I find part of an answer, 'You know how tragedy is supposed to make you find yourself? The theory that I should be stripping away all the layers and finding the real me? But what if there isn't one? I'm so scared that if I peel everything away there'll just be a big empty hole with nothing inside.'

'You're crazy!' says my friendly psychology expert. 'There's plenty inside you—you're just too down to see how real that person is. Trust me; I wouldn't choose a big empty nothing as a best friend.'

I remember the poem I wrote for Martin. I know now why it was a lie: it was a real person's poem—someone who could lift off the mask and find themselves still there, who could reach deep down inside and touch something vital, something clean and strong. But for me, behind the mask, under the shell—there's nothing. Nothing but the mute emptiness of my mind—the swirling, engulfing chaos of a black hole.

I write it again.

I am
peeling like an onion—
decaying slimy layers,
hiding blackened mush inside.

I am
opening like a babushka—
the painted dolls are broken;
there's no baby left inside.

I am
unwrapping like a present—
the paper's torn and crumpled;
the gift's stolen from inside.

Though the 'I am' is still a lie—because now that the superficial Annas have been ripped away there's nothing at the centre except a swirling void, the vortex of fear. The real Anna doesn't exist.

The letters on Dad's desk weren't just about what's wrong with me. They were about what we're supposed to do about it. Suing. Lawyers. Court. Judge and juries. Me on trial.

'It won't be for a couple more years,' Dad says—*as if that makes a difference . . . as if I could hang around for two more years with this as the prize!*—and suddenly anger jolts me out of the greyness.

'I don't want to make money out of this! It's putting a price on my body—it's obscene—it's prostitution! I don't know how you can do this to me!'

'I'm not doing anything to you!' *Dad's shouting too; first time he's been angry at me since the accident.* 'You've got serious problems, you seem to be in constant, terrible pain; the doctors are suggesting that you'll only ever be able to work part-time if at all—you're going to need some extra money to make up for that!'

'I just don't see why I should have go to court ... as if I were the criminal!'

'It wouldn't be like that. But Anna, I'm your father; I'm an accountant—this is the one thing I can do for you. Let me do it.'

The suffocating blackness again; fighting the terror by screaming myself awake. What if I didn't? *What if I let the choking win?*

Luke wants to walk by the river after English; I tell him my foot's too sore. I need more than a muddy path, more than a giant log and damp trees to make me feel alive again. His eyes are dark and his face worried; for once he's got nothing to say.

I'm dragging my friends down with me. They'd be better off I were gone.

My neck is cramping and tearing, the pain on the back of my head is screaming, and I might too if it doesn't stop. I'll have to take a painkiller.

So what am I waiting for? There's nothing magic about my birthday; I'm not going to have a miracle in the next ten days. I'm not going to have a miracle ever. This is it, this is as good as it gets: pain and failure, failure and pain. It's not living, I'm not alive, I'm nothing but a blob of pain and I can't keep going this way.

They're gone—all of them, the pack in my drawer and the ones in the medicine cupboard. Find Mum.

'One or two?' Mum asks, doling them out as if I were a kid. *I don't believe it—she's hidden my tablets!*

'They're powerful drugs,' she says. 'We shouldn't keep them where Matt could get them.'

Except that the bathroom cupboard has a childproof lock—Matt can't open it. And he knows that if he went through my underwear he'd need more than painkillers to help him.

'You took them out of my drawer! What happened to privacy—or did I lose that along with everything else?'

Mum flares as fast as me; suddenly we're both screaming. 'I'm worried about my child's life and you complain about *privacy*!'

Then just as suddenly she's crying. So am I. Crying with messy tears and drippy nose and lots of noise. Because I know which child she means. The one that can open childproof locks. The one who might have been looking for a way out.

And I know I can't do it. I can't hurt them that badly.

'It's okay, Mum, I promise. I won't do anything. Promise.'

It's not that easy. It was always there, a talisman to touch when life was unbearable, that secret plan—the escape route. Now even that's gone. With no way out the pain is infinite, misery can go on without end. One more bit of control lost. But I promised. Some promises you can't break.

(HAPTER 12

Part of the promise is agreeing to see a counsellor. Counsellor doesn't sound as bad as psychologist. Not as crazy.

Her office is in a big old house, behind Mario's Hair and a beautician (*we fix your head, inside and out*). I pretend I'm here for my usual trim of split ends and fringe, but I've never felt this sick waiting for Mario. It's almost a relief when a woman appears and asks me to follow her down the hall.

She's about thirty, with a lively face that stills to concentrate as if what you're saying is the most important thing she's ever heard. Her name's Laura and she says that it's my time, to talk about whatever I like, and that nothing I say will leave the room. *What if I said I wanted to kill myself? Would she just keep quiet and let me?*

I don't know what I'm supposed to say.

So she asks me about the accident; how it happened, what it was like being in hospital. I can tell her all that; I describe the pain and the bitch battles with the nurses and the old lady dying. I tell her that one of my best friends couldn't deal with it, and how she dumped me.

'That's a pretty terrible story,' Laura says. 'Some people might even want to cry about it.'

Maybe they would. Some people aren't me.

I go on with my story—part of the promise was that I'd co-operate, not just turn up—the doctors' visits; the tests. I tell her that I've been told I can't do just about everything in the world that's important to me.

But I don't tell her how I feel about it. I tell it as if it's somebody else's story—just the facts—no emotion. I can't take the risk. Can't tell her how scared, how *terrified* I am that if somebody gets right into my head, pokes around and tears it apart, it might never come back together again.

She's quiet for several minutes when I finish.

'You didn't want to come here today, did you?' she says at last.

Not much point in lying.

'You've been through hell, and it's not over yet. You've had extraordinary adjustments to make, not just in your life now, but in how you see the future—I suspect you can't picture it at all at the moment . . . am I right?'

If I could see a future I wouldn't be here!

'You'd be crazy if you weren't sad about all this.'

I'll risk one question: 'So if I'm not crazy—why do I sometimes say that I died in the accident?'

'What do you think?'

'Because the old me is dead?'

'The old you is dead,' she repeats. 'That's a very powerful statement, and might well be the reason you feel that you died. But your problem now—your task—is to find the new you, and we've got three options on how you'd like to work at that: we can set up regular appointments for you to come and see me; if you don't think you can work with me, I can refer you to someone else; or I can simply give you the names of a few books and a couple of suggestions and leave it at that. If you don't feel comfortable about starting therapy there's no point forcing it on you—it has to be your decision.'

If I talked to any psychologist it'd be her . . . but, 'It seems so weird—coming in to spill your guts once a week!'

She laughs. 'When you put it like that . . . What's weirder is that when you're ready, it works. So any time you feel really desperate, or you'd just like to talk, I'll be here. Please call me.'

She means it. It's me I'm not so sure of.

'One more thing,' she adds, as I'm getting ready to go. 'There are two ways of crossing a chasm: you can walk a tightrope without looking down—you tried that, and it didn't work. It never really does. The other way is to work your way down and up the other side—but you've got to get to the bottom first.'

Is there anywhere further down to go?

'But you're going to make it,' she adds. 'It mightn't be exactly the way you planned, but you'll make it.'

'An un-birthday present,' Luke announces, and pulls a walking stick from behind his back.

I'm nearly over my fantasy of my stick being neon—but this one really is. It's been painted white and then completely covered with red and black designs that look like Chinese characters.

'They are'—and he starts pointing them out—'yin-yang, Tai Chi, peace, strength, love. They're the only ones I know—I had to repeat them a few times.'

'Does it glow in the dark too?'

'Of course. But the siren's optional.'

'And you painted it for me?'

'I just thought—hey, if you're going to use something all the time it should express your personality. If you've got it, flaunt it.'

'I don't think anyone ever said that about walking sticks!' But I look at it again, each character so finely drawn, the total geometric effect of the red/black alternation. I stroke it gently, turning it over and over in my hands—it must have taken hours. 'It's fantastic—thanks.' The memory of the last time I thanked him hangs in the air between us; I look away, forcing myself to stay in my chair, and tell him Laura's theory about the chasm. 'I can't believe I have to feel even worse before I can get better!'—*trying to make it sound like a joke; hearing the panic in my voice—she's got to be wrong, because it's impossible to feel worse than I do now.*

'Maybe she just meant that you have to let yourself open up and be honest about how you're really feeling,' says Luke, and his face is so sad and tender that something twists inside me as if I'd kissed him again after all.

The rest of the family have all gone to see Laura now, one after the other. 'Nothing to be ashamed of,' Dad says, 'something like this has to affect all of us.'

Bronny comes home from school hyper with news; I haven't seen her this excited since Dad gave her the stethoscope. Vinita's cousin Rajiv has come to stay; Vinita has to move in with her little sister Charleeni, so that Rajiv can have her bedroom, but Vinita doesn't mind because he's so cool.

'He's from Bondi! That's a really big city and Vinita said he couldn't sleep at first because it was so quiet here.'

'Bombay?' Dad suggests, but it's Bronwyn's story—she gives him a scathing look and goes on with a list of the presents he's brought from the exotic bazaars of Bondi: a real sari for Vinita—and her mum's going to teach her how to wear it, and she might let Bronwyn have a go, but not to bring it home.

Slightly surprised to discover that our house has grown a second storey, I climb a flight of wooden stairs. At the top is a room with a half-open door. Sun is streaming in the window, the wallpaper is a riot of extravagant trees and birds; I understand that it's going to be my new room and I want to go in.

Mrs Hervey is on her hands and knees, scrubbing the floor in front of the open door with an old-fashioned scrubbing brush, lots of water and suds. 'Soon as it's all cleaned out,' she says cheerily, 'you can go inside.'

My hair is too long, too much trouble, *too much the old me*—and it's coming off today. Mario wants to know how I want it; I tell him to do what he likes. He goes on asking till I glance around the room and choose a poster of a soulful-looking girl with dark hair cut in straggly layers. 'Maybe not quite so wispy,' he says, gazing critically at my head in the mirror. 'Your face is too strong.'

My face is a liar.

'You've got beautiful hair,' he adds, disappointed that I don't care more. 'You could probably sell it to a wig-maker if you wanted.'

'No!' *No more bits of me are for sale!*

He gathers up a huge swathe of it in one hand, brandishing an old-fashioned cut-throat razor in the other. *One slip and I won't have to worry about my promise.* 'Ready?' and he slashes—three strokes and a lifetime of hair is gone.

Trimming and shaping takes longer, freeing my ears, shaving up the back of my neck. The hair that's left is a sleeker, darker blonde; the girl that looks back from the mirror looks older—more mature. I like it. In spite of the scars under her eye and mouth, I almost like her. I almost feel good as I pay at reception and start out to meet Mum.

And freeze, face to face with a slight, pale, nervous-looking guy in his early twenties. My stomach cramps as if I've been kicked, sweat suddenly pours down my face and every bit of my body is screaming at me to get away.

'Come on through, Trevor,' Laura calls from down the hall—and as the blind panic pushes me out into the fresh air, I understand.

Mum, reading in the car, leans to push the door open for me, her comment on my hair broken off mid-word as she sees my face. 'You look like you've seen a ghost!'

'Trevor Jones.'

'Oh, Anna.' Her voice breaks as she drops her book to hug me. 'My poor baby. Let's get you home.'

I'm shaking; I think I might be sick. I don't just want to go home, I want to go to bed with a hot water bottle and a cuddle.

'How did you recognise him?' she asks suddenly. 'You didn't regain consciousness till you were in the ambulance.'

Maybe fear has its own memory, stronger than thought. Maybe his face is carved into some hidden pain part of my mind.

'You must have seen him in the car, before it hit,' she suggests, 'and so you remember that even though you've lost the actual impact.'

It's the best explanation either of us can think of.

But I still need to go to bed. Thank God the kids are at school and that it was Mum who took me for my haircut after English; I don't want to be alone and I don't want to be brave.

She sits down on the bed beside me, holding my hand. 'It's a small town—it was bound to happen sooner or later.'

'I know, I've been dreading it—and I know it's best to get it over with,' but I'm crying, crying like a baby, and as I roll onto my front to muffle the tears in my pillow, Mum rubs my back in the same way.

'Come on,' she croons, stroking gently, soothingly; 'come on, you'll be all right.'

And I know I'm here on my bed with my mother comforting me, but now I'm somewhere else as well . . . 'I'm choking!'

'How do you mean?' Mum asks, gently massaging my left shoulder.

'I'm choking! Like I can't swallow.'

She goes on rubbing quietly. 'Just feel it,' she says. 'It might help.'

'It's the seat belt,' I say, and now I can see the me that isn't in my bedroom, the me that's strapped into the seat and the people running around outside the car, panicky. Hayden is there, and another man, white-faced, the man I've just seen. They're rocking the car, 'with a jemmy,' I tell her, 'trying to get the door off,' and as the pitching gets more violent I grab the side of the bed so I don't roll off it and Mum tells me to stay with it, it'll be okay.

Then the rocking stops, changes to a spiralling inside my head, as if my brain is a two-dimensional disc, a frisbee spinning inside my body. And the body in the car is floppy—

'Floppy?' Mum asks.

'The stuffing's come out.' Now I see the black tube leading from the floppy body up out through the car roof and I'm slipping into it.

'Mum, I don't want to die!' But I go on up the black tube; it's tight, squeezy and I don't belong in it. 'I don't want to be here!' Now the body is gone; dissolved into a formless black mass, and all of me is in the tunnel. 'I'm not supposed to be here,' I repeat.

'Where do you want to be?'

'With the people. Outside the car. With Hayden.' Another fear. My body's losing control; I'm going to wet my pants, oh God, worse, please no. Please not that.

Mum's voice is an anchor, a reminder that the story's already happened and that it had a happy ending. 'What's happening now?'

I can't answer. I'm still in the tube. I'm nearly at the end, I can see the light ahead—brilliant, brighter than sunshine, clear and golden—and my head is ready to pop out of the tunnel and into its glow ... Suddenly I'm slipping down, like a rush of water released from a dam, a relief that's so sweet it tears at my insides. 'I'm going back into the body ... I'm there.'

And I know that this is the point where the nightmares begin, the clawing through unconsciousness, fighting the blackness that threatens to swallow me—the blackness that's death. But I don't have to go through that again—I'm back on my own bed with Mum beside me and her arms around me.

I'm shaking, shaking all over, so hard the bed is trembling too, my heels drumming a tune of fear on the bedspread. 'Oh my baby,' Mum says, 'it's okay, you're okay.' She covers me with a blanket, rubs my hands and feet, and cuddles me. She's crying and shaking a little too.

CHAPTER 13

'I don't know why I made up something like that!'

'You know perfectly well you did *not* make that up! Something happened to you that was just too much—no wonder you didn't want to remember! But I guess it's been niggling away at the back of your mind, and when you saw Trevor Jones you couldn't hold it back any longer.'

'Maybe.' I'm still crying, just the occasional tear, it's okay. 'How do you know so much about it?'

'I read the books Lynda lent you,' she says dryly. 'As well as a fair bit of thinking—and talking to Laura.'

'Did you know she was seeing Trevor Jones?'

'No! She keeps everything completely confidential. Just a coincidence that we both chose her.'

'Do you think I'll have to go through that again if something else reminds me?'

'Not from what I've read. The theory is that now you know what your subconscious has been dealing with, you can do what you like with it.'

Do what I like with it. It's a funny way to look at dying, even a mini-dying, but it's good.

'Mum—if the doctors are right I'm never going to be fit enough to do karate again. Or teach phys ed.'

She wipes away tears, flicking them abstractedly across her cheeks with a finger. 'I know.'

'You don't think I'm giving up—letting you down?'

The tears are too strong now to be wiped with one finger. 'Letting us down! Darling, we're *proud* of the way you've fought this, this terrible thing that we'd have given anything— anything at all—for you not to have gone through. But now . . . it's not giving up, it's confronting the truth . . . and right now that's not only the most courageous thing, it's the *only* way you're going to move ahead.'

'I really liked karate, Mum.'

'I know. And maybe nothing will ever take its place. But the real waste would be to so fixated on karate that you never tried anything else that you *could* manage.'

'There'll never be anything that's the challenge karate was.'

'I think your life is enough of a challenge—a more restful hobby mightn't be all bad!'

I smile at that. Mum's still crying. 'At least Mario came up with the perfect job—growing my hair for wigs!' I must still be crying too because now I'm laughing and it sounds hysterical.

'Good thing you've got a year to come up with something better.'

She sits a while longer, her hand on my shoulder, till we've both blown our noses a few times and the tears have stopped. 'I guess I should go. Luke will be wondering what's happened to me.'

'He won't mind. Luke's good.'

'He is. I'm glad you've noticed.'

The memory of that kiss is suddenly so strong that I know I'll blush if I ask her what she means. I put it away to think about when I'm alone.

She's hesitating; there's something important she wants to say. 'That promise you made me . . . now that you know how hard you fought to stay alive, aren't you glad you didn't waste it?'

She's right. The worst of this whole thing has been the total powerlessness, being controlled by my broken body—its pain, its X-rays, diagnoses and bad news doctors. But I was the one who decided to stay alive. And if I won that fight, losing some of the smaller ones doesn't seem so bad. Throwing in the big one now would have been really stupid.

Mum drags Dad out for a long walk as soon as he gets home, sneaking out without dog and kids. I guess this afternoon was a bit heavy for her too.

And for Dad, once he's heard it all. He's very quiet and looks pale, goes straight from the garden to his office and shuts himself in for an hour, reappearing suddenly to give me a hug. 'Thanks for coming back,' he says.

'Wow!' Jenny exclaims. 'That's creepy.'

My throat is dry. It hasn't been an easy phone call, even to her.

'And you could see what was happening around the car?'

'Not while I was actually in the tunnel—then I was just concentrating on not wanting to be there. But before . . . I know how strange it sounds, Jen, but I could see the people running around outside, looking in the windows—and I hated them staring at the poor body when there was nothing she could do about it.'

'Why do you keep saying "the body"? It was you, wasn't it?'

'I guess so . . . it was my body, but it wasn't me. I wasn't in it.'

'I'm just trying to think what you'd be saying if something like this had happened to me.'

'Okay; I'd try to get you to be logical and work out a scientific explanation—but I don't want that now. It's just *there*—I don't need it explained.'

'When you were in the tunnel and said you were supposed to be with Hayden—do you think that's why you're so determined to stick with him?'

'Maybe. It's a pretty powerful sign, isn't it?'

'Powerful sign, bull! You say you'd rather be down on the ground with Hayden than go on up the tunnel and die! It wasn't exactly a win-win situation!'

'You think I was just talking about being outside the car? Like I was saying, "I'm supposed to be alive, like everybody else?"'

'I think if you'd had the dog and cat with you, you'd have said, "I'm supposed to be with Ben and Sally." Think about it.'

So much to think about. I think I've reached the bottom of Laura's chasm—and I've survived. Maybe that was the miracle I was looking for.

I'm even starting to believe the other thing she said—that once I reached the bottom I could start climbing up again. That I was going to make it.

I'd really love to know what Luke thinks about all this.

But a truckload of potting mix arrives at the nursery just as English finishes, so Luke's in a rush to drop me off and sort it out. And Mum wants to be home on my birthday so she's swapped him tomorrow for next Wednesday . . . I won't see him till Monday.

Right now it seems a long time away.

Stuff the potting mix!

'Wine science,' I tell Hayden, dropping the careers handbook as he comes in. 'That wouldn't be bad. I could taste as much as I liked because everyone always thinks I'm drunk anyway.'

But Hayden's wearing his solemn face and my joke doesn't crack it. 'I've been thinking about it too.'

'Wine tasting?'

'Anna, I'm trying to be serious! About next year . . . If you're still going to be in school, I don't know if I should go to Melbourne. I was thinking maybe I should stay here.'

'I thought Yarralong TAFE didn't offer surveying!'

He shrugs. 'I could get a job.'

'Like what? And why? Your marks are okay.'

'Why do you think? Because of you. I want to be here . . .'

Why aren't I feeling mushy? Why isn't this the most romantic thing that's ever happened to me?

'. . . to look after you.'

Waves of panic and claustrophobia wash over me—*that's why!* I've just started to sort myself out, I can't deal with this right now. I need some space, some time!

A hyperactive eight-year-old charges between us and out to the garden, whirling a collar and leash over his head. 'Ben! Let's practise for school!'

In one second flat, Ben's gone from a peacefully curled-up shape on the back verandah to a whirl of shrilly barking excitement tearing round and round the garden. Every few laps he pauses to lick Matt's hand and his leash before dashing off again.

'The teacher says he's very good,' Matt says proudly. 'He's all the way through Level 1 already!'

'Level 1 must be enthusiasm,' I whisper. Hayden laughs at that, and by the time the noise calms down he has to go. He checks what time we're going out for dinner tomorrow, says he has some shopping to do and leaves.

My panic's gone too, but the vague uneasiness stays. No more excuses; Jenny's right—I have to think about this relationship and why I want it so badly.

The familiar images crowd into my mind; Hayden and me at training—watching him watching me; that last tournament, the incredible feeling of winning, of being a *winner*; Hayden cheering for me; kissing me . . . If you had to choose one moment for your life to be stuck on, that would be mine.

Isn't that exactly what you're doing? asks a nasty little voice.

But that's not all we have. We're more than one kiss, one incredible day. It's Hayden I'm in love with, not being a winner.

It is?

I'm starting to feel panicky again, but I've got to think this through. And push away the thought of Luke, of that other kiss. Sort out one thing at a time.

'Can I go to Vinita's after Anna's opened her presents tomorrow?' Bronny asks.

'Don't see why not,' Dad says, but we're all a bit surprised. The two of them normally spend Saturdays lying in wait for Hayden and thinking up witty things to say that will make him notice them.

Mum's quicker than I am. 'And how's Rajiv settling in?' she asks.

Bronwyn giggles.

Looks like Hayden's been dumped!

Lynda phones in the evening to say an early happy birthday.

'I've got some news too,' she says. 'I'm changing jobs. Guess where I'm going!'

'Health food shop?'

She laughs. 'I thought about it! You know how frustrated I get with conventional medicine. But in the end I figured that's what I know about ... so I'm going to be part of a medical team setting up a new hospital in—your dad's going to freak out!—Mozambique. Their health services were pretty well destroyed during the war, and now they're trying to get things running again. And it's incredibly beautiful—tropical beaches, coconut palms ...'

'That's fantastic! When do you go?'

'January. Now hand me over to my dear conventional brother. I'm not sure he'll agree with "fantastic".'

But Dad surprises us. He says of course he'll worry and he doesn't believe one word about her being sensible. He also says it's her life and he can understand that she wants to accomplish something in it. 'Good for you, Lynda,' he says. 'Get out there and do it.'

Wake up this morning and I'm an adult! A grown-up. One day older and I'm old enough to vote, drink, drive and sign my own disclaimers.

Mum and Dad are clearly worried that I might crack—the reminder that the best of my life is over instead of beginning might send me back down into that black hole of gloom.

But I've had enough of cracking—there's only so much falling apart you can take before you have to start putting it all back together again. And I know exactly how I have to start.

Or I could wait till tomorrow and not spoil my birthday.

Chicken! It's the best present I could give myself. Do it and get it over with, so we can all get on with our lives.

Bronwyn, carrying the cat, is sneaking into my room, inching the door open to see if I'm awake. *(She doesn't seem to have any bandages on! Something's worked for her—maybe it will for me too.)* 'Sally wants to say happy birthday.'

They both snuggle in with me. Matt follows a second later, bouncing, wiggling . . . time to get up.

The kitchen table's full of presents, flowers and cards—aunts, uncles and friends, everyone's remembered this year. I'm not sure if it's just because it's my eighteenth, or if it's a way of saying they're glad I stuck around for my birthday.

Why do people say 'when I get old' and 'if I die'? Don't they know it's the other way around?

A beautiful jumper from Mum and Dad. Body Shop bath oil from Bronwyn (sounds like a B sentence from 'Sesame Street'), a nailbrush shaped like a pig from Matt, an aromatherapy kit from Lynda, a heap of twenty- or fifty-dollar notes from other aunts and uncles and Nan and Pop. (None of them have heard of not sending cash in the mail.) Nothing from Oma and Opa—they must have spent their money on phone calls, talking to Mum for so long that she complained her throat hurt from speaking so much Dutch.

The phone goes again now and Jenny sings 'Happy Birthday' into my ear.

'Fashion Girl's having a sale—do you want to check it out, since you're all cashed up?' It used to be a regular Saturday-morning thing—Jenny, Caroline and I wandering around the shops, trying stuff on that we knew we'd never buy—laughing ourselves sick and dreaming about the day when we'd have some real money. 'Costa will come if I make him, but the poor guy's heart just isn't in it!'

'Guess it's time I gave him a break. Let's go—shop till we drop!'

Dad looks worried at 'drop' but gets the look from Mum— *'She's finally doing something—don't stop her now!'* I don't think I was supposed to read it, but it's okay. Today everything is okay. I don't even mind that now he's obviously worrying about the bus and trying to figure out how to ask if I'll manage.

'Could you give us a lift in when Jenny gets here, Dad?'

He lightens up so much he has to put on his strict father voice to hide it. 'Oh well ... since it's your birthday.'

'We'll get the bus home—and it's okay, I can manage the step!'

'I'm sure you can,' Dad says dryly.

'Happy birthday, darling,' Mum says, giving me another hug, and for a minute the three of us stand there grinning at each other, with tears in our eyes. It feels as if someone should come up with an incredibly profound statement, something about my being eighteen and alive, and the meaning of life and how I'll discover it in the end.

'Ben's remembered how to sit!' Matt screams, skidding across the kitchen tiles with the dog behind him. 'Sit, Ben! Sit!'

The dog hesitates for a second—and sits.

'Stay!' Matt shrieks, dancing around the table and then out of sight into the lounge room. 'Is he still sitting?'

'Yes!'

'So can he come inside again? Now that he's trained?'

'It looks like it,' Dad agrees.

A confusion of red pyjamas and black fur begins waltzing ecstatically around the floor—the profound statement might have to go unsaid.

A moment's panic when the doorbell rings. It's Jenny's mum, who I've been avoiding since I flushed her book down the toilet, but she just wants to say happy birthday and give me a small quartz crystal. I'm not so sure about the miracles she promises, but it's pretty.

Jenny's got a card and air of suspense, stepping carefully around the collapsed heap of Matt and Ben to admire the presents spread out across the breakfast table and add a tiny package to them. Mum makes another cup of coffee and Bronny leans against my chair to watch me open it; Jenny and I have shared enough Christmases and birthdays for them to know her knack for finding something special.

Silver glints from the tissue paper as I unwrap a pair of earrings. A filigree silver ball dangles on the chain of each one; inside is another filigree ball, and inside that is another, and another and another ... The last one is a tiny silver kernel.

'It's true, you know,' Jenny says. 'There *is* something real inside.'

I hug her, blinking back tears. 'Thanks, Jen.'

'Can you open them up and take out the little ones?' Matt wants to know. Mum quickly retrieves them and drops them back into my hand.

'I think you should wear them always,' Bronny decides.

'So do I; they're fantastic.'

Jenny follows me into the bedroom, where I stop playing with them for long enough to put them on, admiring the way they twinkle out from under the new, springy layer of hair. 'The new Anna!'

Dad drops us at the door of Fashion Girl, at the start of the mall. I'd forgotten how close and crowded the shop was; how daunting the rows of clothes can be when you don't know what you want. I'm not ready for decisions, the finality of choice, and let myself be sucked into the whirl of Jenny's enthusiasm in her quest for my new look. Jeans, sweaters, baggy silk pants with flowing jackets, slinky after-five dresses, tiny kilts and A-line mini-skirts—if it's there, try it on, is Jenny's motto. Her final choice is a feathery, sleazy purple number that make us giggle so hard the sales assistant sticks her head in to ask how we're going. ('And when?' adds the look.) 'Perhaps if you could decide whether you're looking at sports wear or evening apparel,' she snaps, 'it would be easier to find something to suit.' She flips the bundle of clothes off its hook and closes the curtains with a snap.

'We've been told,' whispers Jenny. 'You think we should crawl out and beg forgiveness?'

'Suits me. Crawling's good—not so far to fall!'

'As long as you don't land on her "evening apparel".'

The woman watches us leave, glaring again as I stumble against a swaying rack of new season's shirts when my stick catches the base. Maybe she thinks it's the fashion statement of a slightly crazy adolescent—which is the best birthday present a cranky sales assistant could give me.

Jenny leaves me to have a rest for the afternoon; she'll be back later to go out for dinner. It was my choice—going out for a romantic dinner with Hayden, Jenny and Costa, or the whole family plus Hayden and Jenny. I chose the family night. *Had my subconscious already decided?*

Go ahead and do it. It's the right thing, it has to be done—has to be done now. Just pick up the phone and do it!

'Can you come over?'

'Is something wrong?'

'I need to talk to you.'

Threaten the kids with death if they don't leave us alone. Bronny rolls her eyes and Matt sings his favourite version of the wedding march; Hayden and I go out to the bench under the silky oak.

There's no easy way to do this; all I can do is blurt it out like a speech prepared for assembly.

'It's not working. I wanted to be with you because you're part of the way my life used to be—but I've got to stop pretending—it isn't like that any more. And you're—well, I guess you've got your reasons for wanting to be with me, but it's not love.'

The problem with working scenes out in your head is that the other person isn't always reading the same script. You forget that they might argue.

'Look, I know you've been pretty down lately, but I don't mind; I figure you'll snap out of it sooner or later. I don't care that much about going to parties and stuff anyway.'

'That's not the point!'

'You mean how you're not very interested in—you know?'

'Sex? *I'm* not interested?'

'That sort of stuff,' he mutters. 'But it's okay; that'll work out when you're healthier.'

'We never even kiss! How strong do I have to be?'

'How can I kiss you when I'm so scared of hurting you any more than I already have? All I can think about is what if we're pashing on and I push your neck a bit too far and break it again?'

Finally—the truth. 'That wouldn't happen,' I say more quietly, my anger dying in the face of an overwhelming sadness, for him, for me, for the people we used to be.

'Maybe—but just hurting you'd be bad enough! I've seen you when your neck goes into spasms—I'm not going to risk causing that.'

'So why are we going out?'

'Because ... look, it's your birthday and I care about you—isn't that enough?' *and he looks so hurt I almost want to change my mind, but I can't, pity is not what a relationship is supposed to be about. On either side.*

'I've thought a lot about this, Anna—I really mean it.'

I can't do this! Too hard, too hard ... but I know I'm right. 'Hayden, we've been through a lot together and I'll always care about you—but we never really had a relationship. Maybe we would have if the accident hadn't happened; maybe it would have been great. But it's not—it's no good for either of us. We've got to break up.'

He gets up from the bench, shoulders tensed. 'You know your problem, Anna? You want everything to be perfect. We could have had something good if you'd just given it a try!'

The anger takes me by surprise. So does the present—a small square box with the jeweller's gift wrapping—and the kiss. I'm crying as he turns out of the driveway, but I've lost the last tiny doubt that this was the right thing.

Despite the death threats, Bronny and Matt are both plastered to the family room window. 'Anna and Hayden sitting in a tree,' Matt begins to chant. 'K-I-S-S-I-N-G.'

'Great; you can spell. Where's Mum? I've got to tell her Hayden's not coming for dinner.'

CHAPTER 14

Luke's waiting for me after English. It's the first day of spring, and a re-run of the first time he picked me up—the rest of the world disappears and all I can see is Luke, in jeans and a denim shirt, leaning against the car in the sun.

Luke! How could I have been so stupid? His name sings in my head; my body's flooded with the feelings that I've been trying to hide since the day I kissed him. Half of me wants to run and throw myself into his arms and the other half wants to disappear in the opposite direction because I don't think he could ever feel the same way—*did he kiss me back, or was he just being kind?* I tell myself to act natural but by the time I reach the car I can't remember what natural is.

He asks about my birthday, and I mumble some answer without really looking at him. I'll just have to learn to deal with my feelings—shove them down, push them away—because the worst thing of all would be not being able to talk to him any more.

We get to the house and he follows me in.

'Your hair's so different!' he says suddenly. 'I mean, you look great—but didn't it feel strange, having it cut?'

'Not as strange as what happened afterwards.' And I tell him the whole story; I'm not quite as cold and shaky as when I told Jenny, but it's still not easy. I get up to stare out the window at the bees buzzing around the knot garden. 'The near-death experiences I've heard about on TV always sound peaceful and happy—but I hated this. I just didn't want to be dead! I felt so sure that I wasn't supposed to be in that tunnel—I was supposed to be with Hayden, outside the car.'

'You must love him a lot,' he says gently, 'to fight your way back to be with him.'

'I think it was the other way around. I thought I loved him because I wanted to be alive—I wanted to be one of the people outside the car, not the body they were trying to help! And later . . . I think it was part of wanting to be the same person I'd been before; pretending the accident hadn't happened.'

He's standing behind me, looking out over my shoulder, so close my body forgets it ever felt cold and terrified. 'When did you realise all this?'

'Friday night. I broke up with him on Saturday.'

'But didn't he buy you a ring?' he asks, his arm around my shoulder cuddling me so gently I almost think I've imagined it; I shake my head—realise I'm holding my breath, waiting to see what will happen, but then both his arms go around me and as I lean back against him his cheek is against mine, and nothing has ever felt so right.

And now somehow we're on the couch, and when I can breathe again the last of the doubts have disappeared. He's not afraid of hurting my neck, either. In fact I think we've just discovered a new cure for pain.

He pulls away for a second to look at me, framing my face in his hands. 'Last Friday night I saw him in a jeweller's shop . . . I've spent the last three days wondering what you were going to tell me today.' His face is pressed against my throat; I can feel his breath and the movement of his lips as he speaks; it feels as if his words are soaking straight into my skin. 'I listened to you, describing your dying . . . I'm trying to understand it, I want to feel what you've been through . . . but I can't, it's too much; I don't even know how to help you deal with it. You've been facing death, while I was worrying that I couldn't take it if you said I was going to lose you—and that this,' running his hands over my shoulders, undoing my tie and the top button of my white school shirt, 'was never going to happen.'

'You've thought about it before?'

'God, Anna! You don't want to know how much!'

Another long kiss, his weight pressing me into the couch, and when our tongues meet this time it's the most intimate, exciting thing I've ever felt. My mouth thinks it should go on forever, parts of me want to find out what else could happen— and my mind figures that this morning I didn't even know I was in love with the guy and sleeping with him this fast would be pretty tacky.

'I'd better get ready for physio.'

'I could help,' he offers, his hands on the next button.

I do it up again. 'I don't think that's the word you want.'

'You might be right,' he admits, and eventually lets me get up.

I'm bubbling for the rest of the day, so happy I'm surprised Mum and Dad can't read Luke's name imprinted across my forehead, but I'm not quite ready to share him yet. Easier to let them think it's the late birthday card that's made me feel this way.

Oma, Opa and Aunt Cisca are sending me a return ticket to Amsterdam; all I have to do is decide when. 'We know you're not very strong yet,' Cisca writes. 'If you want to wait till next year, when you finish school, that will be okay.'

Happy, excited, grateful—I feel all the things you should when you're handed tickets for an overseas trip, especially the one you've always dreamed of doing.

I'm nearly asleep before it hits me. My dream trip wasn't just getting to Europe—it was about all the things I'd do when I got there, like cycling around Holland. Now I need both hands to keep my balance on the physio's exercise bike.

Suddenly the whole impact of my birthday, that I've been staving off for three days, crashes down on top of me. I don't know if I'll ever do the things normal adults do—don't know if I can learn to drive, no idea at all about what I can do when I eventually finish school ... I'll never even be able to vote if I have to stand in a queue!

Reality is so grey and grim it's hard to remember that I've just had one of the most fantastic days of my life. Hard to decide which feeling is true.

Maybe they both are. Maybe getting better won't be magic; no single experience is going to be the Abracadabra.

'So what's the worst that can happen?' Luke wants to know.

I hadn't thought about it so concretely. 'Just going and not being able to do anything that I wanted ... or being sick on the plane. If I'm so dizzy I can hardly stand after driving to Melbourne, how am I going to be with a thirty-six-hour flight after that?'

'You could always use a wheelchair.'

'A wheelchair! This was supposed to be my dream cycling trip, and you tell me I can go in a *wheelchair*!'

'You know what I think the very worst would be? If you didn't go at all—if you were so scared of not managing perfectly that you didn't try. I never thought you'd let this thing beat you like that!'

'I'm not letting it beat me!' My coffee cup shatters in the sink, brown stains spraying across the tiles; Luke's sucking a splash off his wrist. I can't even remember throwing it.

He's put his own cup down—more gently than I did—and his arms are around me; I didn't know I was crying, but I am; he's telling me to stop, it's okay. 'I just meant,' he says, 'that if that was the worst thing, it'd still be better than not going. And you *are* getting stronger, if you went after school next year, you might manage fine.'

'I won't be cycling, though.'

'Doesn't sound like it. Lousy weather for cycling anyway, Holland in December.' And then we're on the couch again—*seems like there are some things you can do every day and never get bored*—and plane trips and falling over disappear right out of my mind.

'And I could go with you,' he says suddenly, coming up for air.

'To push my wheelchair?' I tease, leaning back in the circle of his arms, precarious and safe, tracing the line of his mouth with my finger for no reason other than that suddenly, amazingly, I have the right to do it.

'If that's all you want.'

Mia calls out something as I'm leaving after English; I forget the rule about not doing two things at once, turn to answer—and crash to the ground. *I never used to think that turning your head and walking were two separate activities!* My kneecaps feel as if they've cracked, and my right wrist throbs.

'Sometimes I think I'd be better off if I *was* in a wheelchair!' I snarl, as Luke starts the car. 'At least I wouldn't fall over all the time!'

Luke doesn't answer, but stops the car near the Coffee Connection.

'You think a *caffe latte* will stop me feeling sorry for myself?'

He takes my hand. 'I've got a better idea if it doesn't.'

'Bad idea on Thursdays.' Dodging vacuum cleaners and mops does nothing for romance—though he's obviously remembered Mrs Hervey, or I suspect we'd be at home now.

There's a whirring noise behind us; sounds like a herd of bikes charging up the footpath. *Can't they see I've got a walking stick? They'll have to get out of my way, it's too hard for me—and they're not supposed to be on the footpath anyway.* If you do it well enough, self-pity can give you a real high.

With a whirr of fluoro spokes, pink and green, they swerve around and past us—two young guys, laughing and shrieking abuse at each other as they race their wheelchairs down the footpath. Frank at the fruit and veg shop races out to the front to shout at them, stops, and stands looking confused. An elderly couple click their tongues and walk on, shaking their heads.

'I don't know what the world's coming to,' Luke whispers, 'disabled people never acted like that in *my* day!'

I start to giggle. I laugh until I fall over again and have to sit on the kerb, and Luke sits beside me with his arms around me and I laugh until I don't know if I'm laughing or crying. But I know I'm ashamed, and I know I'm lucky after all, because no matter what the doctors say I'll never give up trying and hoping, and you can do lots of things in a wheelchair but I'd rather have legs.

And I know I love this man.

I write to Aunt Cisca and Oma and Opa. What a fantastic present; I'd love to come when I finish school next year—Christmas in Holland would be wonderful. Can they guarantee some snow? I'll practise a bit of Dutch so Cisca doesn't have to translate everything.

Seems a bit early to mention travelling with a boyfriend, when Mum and Dad still don't know I have one. But we're going to a movie tonight . . .

'I'm going out with Luke,' I announce at dinner.

'I know,' Mum says, and laughs at the expression on my face. 'Luke comes back from physio looking like Matt at Christmas; *you've* actually been smiling—it wasn't that hard to guess. Anyway, I'm glad you've sorted everything out.'

'Sorted *what* out?' Dad demands. 'You've broken up with Hayden; now you've got a date with Luke, which for reasons best known to herself, your mother thinks is wonderful. Or is there something I'm missing?'

'No, Dad—that's about it.' I keep a straight face till he leaves the room.

'I think,' Mum says, 'your father saw some advantages in his little girl going out with a boy who was obviously terrified of touching her. Luke's a man—and he's not afraid of much.'

Mum's actually better at straight talking than I am. I can feel myself getting redder.

'I probably don't look at things in quite the same way—and I've seen you and Luke together more than your dad has; honestly, Anna, I sometimes despaired of how long you were going to keep Hayden dangling around the house like a wet blanket! But take it easy. You're such good friends that things could move quickly . . . if it's right, it won't hurt to go slow. You've got all the time in the world.'

Jenny's so happy for me she's crying.

That's what she says—it looks more like she's lying across my bed sobbing her heart out. I didn't think people cried quite like that for happiness. After five minutes I'm sure of it.

'Come off it, Jen—what's wrong?'

'I didn't want to tell you when you were so happy!'

I feel sick. Jenny and Costa always seemed perfect together; they're my standard of what love should be. 'Have you guys broken up?'

'I don't know! It's his parent's twentieth anniversary on Sunday and all the rellies are coming down from Sydney for the weekend.'

'You had a fight because you don't want to go?'

'He doesn't want me to! He says everyone will be speaking Greek and I won't know anyone . . . '

'Sounds logical.'

'But it means we're not going to see each other for the whole weekend! Anyway, if he loved me he'd want me to meet them—I think he's ashamed of me.'

'Jen, you're being ridiculous!'

'I'm not! You've got to admit that Costa's about the best-looking guy around—his family's going to expect him to have a really gorgeous girlfriend. Look at me—short, fat and mousy.'

'His family thinks you're great! And come off the fat bit—at least you've got boobs. But you're special, Jen; you're so warm and open and happy, people feel good around you—isn't that more important than looking like a model?'

'Not to guys.'

Bastard, bastard! I scream silently at Costa. 'Jen, do you think maybe you both just need a little space?'

'We didn't use to want space!'

She goes on crying. I feel incredibly helpless.

'Do you want to spend the night?' I suggest at last, and she sniffs a yes.

Costa arrives an hour later. He looks so tense and unhappy that I don't slam the door in his face after all. Jen disappears with him.

'I thought Jenny was spending the night?' Dad asks.

'She had to go out.'

Mum looks anxious. 'I'm not covering for your friends spending the night with boyfriends.'

'Jenny wouldn't do that!' Dad splutters. 'Would she?'

'Of course not,' I say hopefully, and eventually the doorbell rings again. Costa waves and shouts goodnight; Jenny comes in, looking washed-out and happy.

'What happened?'

'Everything's okay.'

'I guessed that!'

'You were right about space . . . you remember how I was afraid that if we made love I'd be so committed that I'd sort of lose myself?'

'You did it?'

'Mm; Tuesday night.' She doesn't look embarrassed, just private. 'And now it's actually happened, he's the one who was scared by how much he felt—he thought we should just back off for a bit.'

'And?'

'And then he started thinking about not seeing me for a whole weekend, and started imagining how he'd feel if I broke up with him . . . '

'So you're going to the party?'

'Looks like it. He says we're going to be together a long time, and I'll have to meet his crazy relations sooner or later.'

Mum and Dad are going out for dinner and I'm babysitting. They've both been a bit frayed around the edges lately, and some of the snapping and bickering makes Matt and Bronny's arguments sound adult—an evening out on their own might do them some good.

'What kind of cake did you make?'

Mum looks confused.

'It's the first time you've left me alone with the kids since my accident.'

She blushes. 'As a matter of fact, I *did* make a chocolate apple cake. It was a new recipe I wanted to try. Let me know what you think.'

'Can we have it now?' Matt wants to know the instant the front door closes.

'We have to have dinner first,' Bronny says primly. She's in her 'help look after Matt' mood. I wish she'd just be more like a little kid and let me be the grown-up.

I start the kettle and rip open an instant pasta meal. 'Okay, dinner first. Then we can have cake for dessert, or we can build a bonfire and have cake outside.'

I say 'or', but the bonfire's not an option. It's happening. 'We'll build it in that new bed Mum's just dug up.'

Bronny starts to look excited in spite of herself. Matt's ready to explode. I set him to work scrunching up newspaper till the microwave timer goes and he can bolt down his pasta.

We get torches, Matt's newspaper, kindling and firewood. I'd rather rip up a few small trees, giant branches, build a huge pyramid of conflagration. A Hindu funeral pyre.

It starts slowly; I throw on more kindling—I want it to crackle and roar. Matt throws on the Saturday *Age* and nearly smothers it. I poke around till it begins to look like a bonfire.

'Sit further back and don't put anything on for a minute—I need something from the house.'

Butcher's knife from the kitchen, and out to the carport. Hold the elastic cord with one hand; slice with the other. It's not easy to cut; takes a minute to chop through both ends. The fire's going nicely by the time I get back. Bronwyn and Matt are staring.

'That's your new punching bag!'

'Not any more.' And I drop it on the fire.

'It stinks,' says Matt.

'What're Dad and Mum going to say?'

I don't really care. This is for me. This is an exorcism. But anything I could have said is drowned out by a boom like a gunshot. Bits of red leather, cord, and plastic shower down on us. Ben tears around the garden, trampling the flower beds and yapping like a puppy; Matt is shrieking with excitement, dancing his own primitive fire dance. Bronwyn snuggles up to me, 'I guess you did that because you're not allowed to hit it any more.'

We watch the flames a little longer. They're dying down; I push them up with the rake. A siren wails in the distance.

'Here comes the fire truck!' Matt screams. 'The fire truck, the fire truck!'

But the wailing is disappearing into the distance.

'Too bad, Matt. I'll do better next time.' But I remember the cake, which we never did bring outside, and he cheers up again.

Can't skip baths after that smoke, but eventually I get them into bed. I'm tired, but still revved—I've done the wrong thing, and it feels great. I'm still up when Mum and Dad get home.

'Kids behave themselves?'

'Even Matt. And the cake was a three-star. How about you?'

'Wonderful; we'll have to do it more often.'

I'll wait till morning to tell them about the punching bag.

I hadn't expected to speak to a machine, but maybe the message is easier this way; machines don't ask questions. 'Sensai? It's Anna Duncan. I won't be coming back to karate. I just phoned to say goodbye.'

I'm crying, though, when he rings back a few minutes later. *After all this time of holding them in, tears flow so easily now I feel like an ornamental fountain.*

'What's this about quitting? I'd heard you were doing quite well.'

I explain a bit of the doctors' bad news—the precarious vertebrae, the wobbly balance. 'So I'm getting better, but it looks as if there're some things I'll never be able to do.'

'I can't believe it. For someone so fit—it's a tragedy. Bloody awful luck.'

'I'm getting used to it.'

He forces a little jollity into his voice. 'And how's that young man of yours?'

'We broke up last week.'

'Shit. Excuse me while I change feet.'

'It's okay, truly; it was the best thing for both of us. I wish he'd go back to training, though.'

'You and me both. But look, we can't have you just slipping out of karate like this . . . tell you what, barbecue at the dojo, Friday week. Right?'

'Yes, Sensai.'

This is the third time I've been to hydrotherapy. I meet the physio at the indoor pool and when I've finished my exercises I can have a swim.

Tried freestyle the first time—one lap and the building was spinning. The ladder spun out from the wall as I grabbed it—looked again—both rungs still firmly set in concrete.

And when your body starts lying—I mean, real, full-on Academy Award performances about what's happening outside and what's in your poor screwed-up head—you learn a whole new meaning of terror.

Brian hauled me out and dumped me unceremoniously on a bench against the wall. 'I forgot what turning your head does to you! You might give freestyle a miss till the dizziness settles down.'

Breaststroke wasn't much better—three strokes and I couldn't lift my head out of the water. But pain's easier to beat than dizziness, and I'll get stronger . . . four strokes next time.

But backstroke I can do! I've done three laps and Brian says I have to stop, but I could do more if he let me. 'Next week,' he says. 'Don't want to overdo it too soon.'

Once I'm out of the water my ankle hurts so much I can barely hobble to the changing room, but as I sit on the floor of the shower stall, too wobbly to stand, I feel fantastic. I've never liked swimming much, but I think I could learn to.

Martin's pleased with my English work. 'You obviously made the right decision, dropping the other subjects,' he says, 'but your concentration's improved too. Life's looking up, is it?'

'You could say that.'

'Oh God, romance! I should have known. Anyway, if you can get your mind out of the gutter for a moment—'

'It might be a very spiritual romance, Martin!'

'With that look on your face? Anyway, have a look at this—you're not the only one who's been working hard lately.' He tosses a fat manila folder onto the table—'Six Months at Sea,' by Martin Weiss.

'You've finished!'

'I was wondering . . . ' (*Martin, shy and embarrassed?*) 'um, would you read it before I send it to a publisher . . . tell me if it sounds all right?'

'I'd love to.'

'I was thinking, too—this might be the sort of thing you could consider for the future.'

'Round-the-world sailing?'

'Very funny. Editing—books or magazines. You've got a good ability to analyse stories; a reasonable feel for words—and editors don't need to run around much, I wouldn't think.'

'But I don't really like reading!'

'It was just a thought.'

'Did you start caring about me because you felt sorry for me?' We're on the track by the river, the same one we took when I first got a stick, but whether it's holding hands or the orthotic in my shoe, it doesn't seem nearly as rough today.

'No.'

'You didn't feel sorry for me?'

'Of course I did! I'd have had to be inhuman not to. But the first time I saw you, in that split second before I registered the mess you were in, it was as if I recognised you—nothing to do with when you were twelve, just a feeling of "so there she is", like something I'd been waiting for. Then I noticed all the rest of it, and realised how awful it was and how you hated it—but that was nothing to do with the way I felt in that first instant.'

I wish that I could say something as wonderful back to him, but it wouldn't be true. I didn't recognise him; I just thought he was nice. And I felt comfortable with him. Though I used to think about his eyes, and his voice, and his hands . . .

We've reached the log; far enough to sit down. 'Do you want to know when I first . . . when I should have known how I felt?'

'Please,' he says, so softly, so gently, that it twists inside me, and I have to kiss him before I can go on.

'The first day you picked me up at school. You looked so sexy . . . I felt unbelievably happy . . . '

'And you still persisted in going out with Hayden. And I encouraged you.'

'You were noble.'

'I was an idiot.'

'We were both idiots.'

'We'll have to make up for our mistakes somehow.'

Mid-September's not bad weather for a barbecue, warm enough for people in jeans and windcheaters and still too cold for mosquitoes and flies. The park behind the dojo actually belongs to the football club, but the gas barbecues and wooden picnic tables are so convenient that we think of them as ours. (*Thought* not *think*. This isn't mine any more; this is the past.)

Luke's with me—because I like being with him; not because I've got anything to prove. Well, maybe a tiny bit. Whatever way you look at it, my new life is not that great—I might as well show off the one good bit of it.

Everything's a bit stiff at first; I haven't seen most of these people for nearly eight months, and nobody knows what to say. A couple of guys, sounding slightly amazed, tell me that I look great; one's honest enough to say that when he'd heard I had to quit he'd thought I'd look worse. 'But it's brain damage, is it?' he asks innocently. 'I guess that doesn't show.'

Luke squeezes my hand as I mumble defensively about my neck and ankle. (*So what am I saying—it's okay to break bones, but somehow immoral to bump your head? As if it was my choice?*) 'But I guess the head injury didn't help,' I add, and quickly escape to get a drink.

Luke thinks I need a kiss more than a coke.

'What's that for?'

'Being brave.'

'I handled that really badly! Why do I have to feel sick whenever anyone says the words 'brain damage'? The poor guy didn't want to know all that stuff about my neck and my foot—he was just trying to be polite!'

'Tough,' says Luke. 'People shouldn't ask heavy questions if they don't want the answers.'

Sensai gives me a hug; I'm introducing Luke as I see Hayden pull up in his car and sit for a moment as if deciding whether or not to get out.

'He's come back to karate?'

'Coincidence, isn't it? I phoned and told him about this— said it could be a farewell for him too, if he couldn't make it back. Next Tuesday, there he was at training as if he'd never been away.'

He's so obviously pleased with himself that I can't help laughing. 'I'm glad.'

'Best thing for him. You're obviously getting on with your life; he ought to do the same. Now, speaking of getting on with things, we've got a little presentation to make.'

I hate this. Everyone stops talking and gathers around while Sensai hands me a small, heavy, wrapped present and makes a speech about my skill, my contribution to the club, how sorry they are to see me go. He's a bit stilted; the phrases are cliched—and suddenly my eyes fill with their treacherous tears and I'm incredibly moved. I've always felt like I'd snuck out of karate—quit like a yellow belt who can't take the discipline—and this speech, this gift-wrapped leather purse, have given an honourable ending to what was one of the most important things in my life.

Oh, God, they want me to say something too. Now I do hate it. Say thanks—for the present, the evening; for five years of training and companionship. Then incredibly, I hear myself add, 'I've just been through the toughest year of my life, and knowing that I'll never get my black belt has been one of the hardest things in that. But even if it wasn't my choice to leave karate, I'm lucky enough to have found something else' (Hayden winces, and I stumble on quickly, because that wasn't what I meant); 'I'm taking up Tai Chi.'

Luke lifts an eyebrow but nods as if he'd known all along. It's not till we're in the car that he asks if I just made that up so no one would feel sorry for me.

'No; I really want to. It's just—I liked the competition in karate; I really liked knowing I was best; winning.'

Luke unbuckles his seat belt, leans over and kisses me, long and sweet. 'Who won that?' he asks.

'*What?*'

'Not everything good's a competition,' he says smugly, and starts the car.

CHAPTER 15

'You don't exactly know me—I'm the driver of the car that hit yours last January. Trevor Jones.'

The phone slips out of my hand.

'I guess it's a bit late,' he goes on, 'but I thought maybe I should apologise—you don't know how bad I feel. I have nightmares about it.'

My voice comes out in a croak, a cross between a whisper and a cry. 'So do I.'

This seems to encourage him. *Doesn't he realise that* he's *my nightmare?* He picks up speed, 'I went to see this psychologist . . . anyway, I figured I might get over it if I met you. If you felt you could.'

This is too much! It's not fair; it's way too much! 'I don't know.' Damn, I'm crying again, and he'll be able to tell. I don't want him to know but I can't talk, my voice is gulpy. And I'm remembering how I felt last time I saw him; just talking to him now and I'm shaking, heart pounding, cold and sick to my stomach. *But I don't have to take it.* 'I don't think I can. I'm sorry.'

'Oh. Yeah, okay, no worries. Can I leave you my number, in case you change your mind?'

My brain's so numb I write the number down obediently, and don't tear it into tiny pieces until I've hung up.

Trevor Jones wants me to solve his nightmares! What about me—I'm supposed to be the victim here! And maybe I used to think I was strong, but that's one thing the accident's taught me—I'm not nearly as strong as I thought. There are some things I just can't do, and this is one of them.

'What an unbelievable bloody nerve!' Dad explodes. 'Let me speak to him next time he tries to harass you!'

'He wasn't harassing me, Dad! He was trying to say he was sorry.'

I think I've seen my father rant and rave more in the last nine months than in the whole rest of my life, but this time he's really lost it—watery eyes, pinched nostrils and his face fading from grey to white, as if all the blood is being syphoned off by hate.

'Nearly a year later and he suddenly reckons he's *sorry*? Does he think a bunch of roses is going to fix what he did to you?' He slams out of the room.

'Why can't Dad let me deal with my problems myself?'

'He feels so helpless,' Mum says apologetically. 'Somehow as a parent you think you're always going to be able to protect your children.'

'When he acts like that I feel as if I'm supposed to protect him! He looked like he was going to have a heart attack!'

Luckily Jen phones before war breaks out between Mum and me as well. She listens more calmly than Dad.

'It might be good,' she says cautiously. 'Talk about facing your fears! But you'd want to be feeling pretty together to start with or you could just freak out—or knowing you, *freeze* out—so busy making sure you didn't get hurt that you wouldn't feel anything at all and the whole thing would be wasted.'

What can you say to a friend who knows you that well?

'But if you could do it, it'd be an incredibly powerful experience.'

'To tell you the truth, Jen, I've had about enough powerful experiences lately.'

She ignores that. 'I know you're not religious, but forgiving might be a very healing thing to do—you might get more out of it than he does.'

'I've tried bargaining; it doesn't work. There's no one up there handing out happy face stickers for every good deed.'

'Okay; so it's more complicated than that—but it's not as simple as you think either.'

I figure Luke will agree with Jenny. But my clear-eyed, philosophical, what's-the-worst-that-can-happen man is afraid for me and almost as angry as my father. 'It'd be different if *you'd* decided you needed to face him,' he keeps saying. 'Why should you sort out *his* nightmares?'

We're sitting on the bench in the back garden, as close as two people can sit, with his arm around me and my hand resting on his thigh. Funny how comforting it is to touch each other, even when we're not being passionate. And it lets you know what's being said beneath the words, as if another layer of meaning seeps through our bodies and straight to our hearts, so that when I say I don't think I could handle it and Luke adds, 'You've been through enough!' the other level is saying that it's time to forget all this junk from the past and just get on with our lives. But there's another layer even below that, a sad, desperate layer where we both know that Jenny's right and no matter how horrible it is, I've got to deal with that stuff if I'm ever going to be free of it.

But not right now. Right now there's the kaleidoscope of tulips swaying in the breeze, the stubbled line of Luke's jaw and the warm fresh smell of him when I bury my head in his shoulder. The past can wait till I'm ready.

The last trace of yellow has disappeared from my breasts. If I stand naked in front of my mirror now I see a tall slim girl with small, neat white boobs and slightly bony hips—not 'Sun and Surf' material, but nothing to be ashamed of. I don't think anyone who happened to see them would scream in horror any more.

'We've got to talk about next year,' Luke says, as we go out the back gate and down the path to the river. A shiver runs through me; he sounds so solemn, the words so ominous—and feeling the tremor, he squeezes my hand gently and pulls me closer to his side. 'Idiot. It's nothing bad.'

But it is. He's decided to do massage therapy. It's a part-time course in Melbourne for thirty months.

'That's three years!' I feel as if my world has ended; I can't even remember the claustrophobia that swamped me when Hayden wanted to stay in Yarralong next year; now all I want is for Luke to do the same thing. 'Are we breaking up?' *So that's why it's called breaking up, because it tears you in two, shatters your heart and mind and body into tiny pieces.*

'I won't go if it means that,' he says, pulling me down to sit on the ground beside him, and I'm staring into the river without seeing anything but he's cupping my face in his hands, turning me gently round to face him. 'I love you, Anna! But I've got to get on with the rest of my life too. And since I've met you I've started to believe that maybe I could accomplish something more than a few hours in your mum's nursery.'

'What about taking me to physio?'—which I meant to be a joke, but he answers the desperation and the unsaid words, which are not about going to physio, but the time in between school and appointments, when we used to have coffee and talk, except now we skip the coffee and sometimes the talk.

'It's part-time,' he says, 'I'll only be away three days a week. And it's just a year till you'll be down there too.'

I'm snatched up in a wave of bitterness, hurled down and swamped by it. It's not just a year of my life that's been stolen, but a year of Luke's—because instead of being at uni, together in Melbourne . . .

'We mightn't have been together,' he says quietly. 'If all this hadn't happened we mightn't ever have met again.'

'We would have!' *I don't know which is worse—thinking that we wouldn't have met, or being grateful to the accident.*

We're lying on the bank now, his arm under me; my neck's cramping but I'm discussing the future with the man I want to spend it with and I'm not in the mood for pain to interrupt. But Luke sees, and starts to gently massage the corner between my right shoulder and neck. The rigid muscles begin to melt under his fingers. 'That's so good . . . are you doing massage therapy because of me?'

'Not *for* you. Though it's got to be a bonus if I can help your pain, because I love you, and I can't be happy when you're hurting.' *The word 'love' twists through me, warm as his fingers; powerful, sexy little word.*

'I'd hate it if you were just doing it because of me.'

'But it probably *is* partly because of you. That's just the way it is; you can't come into somebody's life without changing it—what's happened to you has got to affect me. And I might never have known how good it is, using my hands to help someone, if I hadn't known you.'

As long as he remembers where the person's pain is. Right now those magic hands seem to be having trouble finding my neck—and this place is not exactly private. Any minute now Dad and the kids could appear, exercising their well-trained Ben. 'You'd better not use your hands on anyone else the way you do on me!' I try to push him away, and am filled with such a wave of tenderness that I can't, clinging to him instead, feeling the warmth of his body flood into me as he buries his head against my throat.

I can't believe it's the end of school already; two more sessions of tutors and then exams after that.

Martin's off to the Canary Islands next week, to bring a boat back to Sydney for someone whose lifetime dream of sailing from England to Australia sent him to the edge of a nervous breakdown. 'It's something you can't describe—that combination of mind-numbing boredom and fatigue, occasional terror and the unbelievable, empty loneliness when you're out of sight of land,' Martin explains. 'At least this guy was smart enough to swallow his pride and admit he's strictly a weekend, coastal sailor—better than ending up insane or dead, which I'd say were his options.'

His manuscript has gone to a publisher. It was interesting—especially the bits where he actually wrote his story instead of a how-to-sail manual. I don't know if I'd like the fear and loneliness but he seems to have found his own ways to conquer them.

And he thinks I'm well prepared for the exam next week. I got a B− in the mid-terms, and he thinks I should do better in the final; I'll definitely do Lit next year. Besides, people in books are always dealing with some momentous problem—the difference with real life is that they usually solve it. If I read enough maybe I'll eventually get a clue to my own.

Maths still isn't so easy. The deferred mid-term was a C and the best Lisa's hoping for the final is that I'll add a plus to it.

'My dad thought maybe I could do accounting and go into business with him,' I tell her, mostly to see her reaction.

'Sweet,' she says dismissively. 'Let's face it—the only thing accounting has in its favour, as far as you're concerned, is that you can sit down to do it. I think you can find a better reason than that for your aim in life.'

Speaking of aims in life, she's going back to full-time teaching next year. 'So I won't be able to do any tutoring—I just couldn't have Becky minded again in the evening after being in care all day.'

'What happens if you want to go out for fun?'

She grimaces. 'I'll worry about that if it happens. It hasn't exactly been a problem this year—hey, don't look so worried! Becky's the best thing in my life; did I tell you she's crawling? Oh, look what I just happen to have ... '

A picture of a baby, wearing nothing but a look of intense concentration, crawling after a bright patchwork ball. Unbelievable how six months have changed a passive baby in a pram to this busy, complete little person.

'You know,' Lisa confides, 'people say there's no such thing as an accidental pregnancy—well, I'm here to tell you there is. We used contraception—and by the time I realised I was pregnant it was too late for an abortion. God, I was angry—I thought my world had ended! You know, I was twenty-six, I loved my work—I was just tossing up whether to do a masters or an exchange year in England; babies were definitely not on my list! But once I had her, none of that mattered—it's not even making the best of things, I really love being a mother. Amazing how life turns out sometimes.'

Something else I didn't know till today is Becky's birthday—she was born on the 29th of January. I didn't ask what time.

A couple of months ago I couldn't have handled it. *Her life started as mine ended*—melodramatic crap, but it's what I'd have thought. Even now I feel cold at the date—but I can't help thinking what a very busy day that was. God must have been humming—here comes Anna, no, too cranky, send her back; how about a little guilt for Trevor and Hayden, a baby for Lisa and a birthday for Becky—plus several million other people around the world dying, being born, losing their jobs and falling in love.

Everyone's got an attack of busy-ness today. Bronwyn and Matt are digging up their bit of garden; Mum's sorting out the vegetable rack in the pantry, where something's died and gone to plant hell.

'Yuck!' she exclaims, chucking a squishily rotten potato into the compost bucket.

She's getting ruthless. Some rubbery carrots follow, and then an onion sprouting a tall green shoot.

Matt grabs the onion. 'Don't throw it out!' he yells. 'We need it for our garden.'

'Will it grow?' Bronwyn asks.

'It already is,' Mum says. 'Just plant it and look after it.'

'Have you thought about social work?' Jenny asks.

'I don't think having problems automatically makes you good at sorting out other people's!'

'But learning to cope might. You're good with people.'

'*Me?*'

'Don't be stupid! You act as if not being mobile means you don't have anything to offer—remember the night I thought I'd broken up with Costa?'

'I didn't do anything!'

'You kept me sane.'

I'm sprawled on the lawn, gazing up at the sky and the waving branches of the silky oak, heavy with its dark seed pods; the bruised thyme below me scents the air. *Picture of a young woman enjoying the spring sunshine*—as long as you forget that what I actually meant to do was walk across the garden. It was okay until my foot got confused by a twig it thought was a log; it's not a very smart foot.

But this isn't a bad place to lie, now I've got my breath back and checked that nothing's much sorer than usual. Pain's a funny thing anyway. It's still always there, somewhere between a nag and a scream—but suddenly I'm starting to beat it. I can't change what it does to my body, but it doesn't get down into me, into my soul, the way it used to. Maybe that's the difference between pain and suffering. If I never got any better than this, I could still survive.

And I'm going to do more than survive—I'm starting to live! It's hard to see any difference from week to week now, but I'm stronger than I was last month. And after the exams I'm going to Melbourne for a new kind of physio Brian thinks might be useful. 'As long as you're not expecting miracles!' he warned—but I figure everything that helps is a bonus.

Luke's going with me. It runs like a song in the back of my mind, behind everything else that's happening. *Luke's going with me.*

Everyone's happy: Mum and Dad figure I'll be safe in the day because Luke won't let me fall off a tram or lie dead in the street, and the three suburbs between Lynda's and Luke's dad's will keep me safe at night. I'm happy because Luke's going to try and sort things out with his dad—and because we're having a holiday together in Melbourne and I don't think my dad's realised how much of each day I have left after physio.

In the parallel universe I used to fantasise about, Trevor Jones stopped at the sign and a healthy Anna went on with her life. She'd have her black belt now and be gearing up for uni next year. But she wouldn't have Luke.

I've dug deep into myself, because if there's any chance that the horrible theory is right and there's a part of me which likes being injured and stops me from getting better, I need to find it and deal with it. But all I've found so far is the part of me that likes being well—and if there's one thing all those doctors' appointments did for me, it's to say that sometimes the damage is real and there's no point pretending it's not there. Recovering slowly doesn't mean I wanted the accident to happen.

So I'm not betraying myself by enjoying any good things that have happened because of it. I can learn and grow from the experience even if I don't believe it was part of some cosmic training scheme.

'Remember what I tried to tell you about the river flowing around the rock?' Luke asks.

'I've learned to flow?' I tease, shifting my weight against him so that my head's supported by his shoulder, staring at the real river flowing past us. I lift my walking stick across my knees and stroke the coloured figures. 'Tell me again what they say.'

'This is the chi; Tai Chi and yin yang; this one's strength.'

'What are the ones on the handle—a whole row all the same?'

'"Fire in the heart"—love.'

'So when I hold the stick I'm holding love?'

'Even when you're not.' And he grins that grin, the one where he looks down at me and my heart slips and I know why I love him.

Love, he said, and strength. I stroke the handle once more when he leaves, and go in to the phone.

'Trevor? It's Anna Duncan. I'll meet you at the psychologist's office next Friday at two.'

Feel a bit trembly when I hang up; go back to my room and find the poem I wrote for Martin.

The black version is wrong too—if there's nothing inside, it wouldn't hurt so much; there must be someone doing the crying. I write it one last time.

> I am
> peeling like an onion,
> shedding papery protection,
> and superficial skin—
> tearing, skinning, ripping off the layers—
> the firm and curving flesh
> of what onions used to be—
> Peeling onions makes me cry.
>
> Shrinking down to nothing,
> my shells are disappearing
> and there's nowhere left to hide.
> But under all the layers
> —a tiny green shoot sprouting—
> I'm growing from inside.